The Gravel Road

David Stewart Handelman

First Printing Edition, 2021

ISBN 979-8-9853724-5-8

Disclaimer

Other Books by the Author

1. "A New World of Selling Real Estate" A guide for Real Estate Agents

2. "Sentiments" A book of Prose, Poetry and Thoughts

3. "Notes from a Quill" Parchment scratches to soothe the day

4. "Words in Rhythm" Rhymes, Poems and Thoughts to open your heart

5. "Between Spirit and Substance" The silent voice of life

6. "Gems of the Soul"

Dedication

To Judy, thank you for being there for me.

To all my Children and Grandchildren, life is an

adventure, explore to the fullest of your abilities.

Push the limits and reach for the stars.

The Gravel Road

PROLOGUE

On the 36th floor of the Highrise Condominium building on New York's finest Park Avenue address, there were two rather large-built men wearing casual clothing. They were sitting, watching, waiting outside the two large doors. Each man had AR-15's as well as a .45 caliber Colt 1911 automatic handgun strapped to their side. They were ex-military fighters, mercenaries, extremely capable of using their weapons if necessary. The cameras were positioned facing every direction.

The full orange sun was just setting over the horizon beyond the tall 10-foot walnut-stained doors. Jonah was sitting alone in front of the large panoramic plate windows, facing the city skyline on a beige recliner – which was made with soft deer-skin leather – looking out, gazing at the beauty of the skyline of Manhattan, Jonah Knight was staring into space–remembering the gravel road that he traveled so long ago. The road that had brought him here today; to Peter Flagstaff, his mentor and replacement father.

The long road in the past that still haunted him, or did it? Thinking of the past, what happened and how he got here. The more he thought about it, the more he was convinced that he had finally arrived, he was home – and not just physically, but in all entirety of the phrase. The gravel road had stopped to haunt his dreams now. He had slain the last demon lurking in the quiet shadows of his past, faced him head-on. There were no monsters hidden under his bed anymore, keeping him up all night, trying their best to scare him into submission.

"I am Jonah Knight," he declared to himself. "Local Auctioneer from Hays, Kansas. I've been shot, knifed, tortured, poisoned, strangled, and nearly run over by people who wanted to see me dead.

"I survived them all," he mused. "Fuck 'em. Fuck 'em all," he thought to himself. "I'm still here, and you're all dead," he chuckled.

Reminiscing about his past and where it all started, he slowly closed his young, tired eyes. His mind had been a whirlwind of thoughts, his heart a raging storm of emotions. It had been a long and tiring day. Closing his eyes, he made an attempt to clear his mind of all the thoughts it wanted to think, all the things that were troubling and plaguing it, and successfully dozed off, going into a quiet, deep sleep not waking up for a period.

1.

CHAPTER ONE

The early morning haze loomed over the Knight Farm. Jonah Knight stood on the porch of the rundown, two-story farmhouse. One kitchen window was covered with plywood, and the paint was peeling on the entire white exterior. The chipped off exterior gave the farmhouse a haunted outlook, but that was the case with every other farm in the vicinity. The revenue had not been good enough to sustain the families, let alone renovating the farms

His blue eyes were squinting at the line of trucks that roared down the long gravel road past the faded

'Knight Farm' signpost. The dust rose thickly up in the air behind the dusty cars and trucks, rambling and darkening the blue skies above. It had been that way for days now. The air was dense with dust particles so much that it had brought down the visibility to a considerable level.

For years, they had ploughed and tilled the fields for the monetary benefits without thinking twice about the consequences it would bring in due time. And the time had finally arrived. The dirt, which was supposed to be under the feet, was up in the air, causing more harm than it had brought good in the previous years.

The blue skies that they had cherished since the dawn of times were now perpetually covered in dirt, blocking the source of life, not letting it warm the earth, preventing everyone from yielding its warmth and bringing life to the dead land. The winds that lightly caressed the face of ripe crops had now turned completely against them, ripping away their stalks, clawing at their roots.

A black Ford sedan and a large black and maroon Packard led the caravan that left a thick cloud of dust rising from the dirt and gravel road behind it. To complement the dark dust-covered skies, the dirt had accumulated in the air behind the caravan, making it inaccessible to the breathing and heaving humans. The cars and trucks seemed to be covered fully in the dirt as the strong winds howled and rattled the windows.

It was a stark, gray, cold morning on April 4th, 1943 – his eighth birthday. The second year of the worst dry spell in the history of Hays, Kansas, the middle of the famous Dust Bowl. For a farmer, dirt was the best friend he could have ever found. However, the same dirt had had enough of the man's butchering techniques to destroy the fabric of it. Without knowing, he had severed the ties with the only best friend it could find and rely on.

The winds howled fiercely across the plains and farmlands. The huge wall of dust from one of the Black Blizzard covered the lands from California all the way through to New York City and up to Boston. It looked as if the skies would fall down in a heavy drizzle, making mankind pay for their sins, and all hell would break loose over their heads. But the rain had only become a dream of the farmers – a dream that they could see with their open eyes but could not make it come true.

The topsoil had vanished, and the winds howled incessantly. In fact, it was the worst drought in the history of the entire country. The blowing winds reached velocities up to 80 miles per hour at times. The lands were as dry as the sands in the hot desert. The farmlands had turned into barren graveyards of perished crops that once blossomed in the fields.

This part of the country never came out of the great depression of 1929 through 1932, where sadness and despair remained throughout the Midwest. Most of the farmers stayed together to lift each other's dreary spirits, except for the few who were able to save money and were successful. However, there was only a handful of them. The others went bankrupt in their effort to save their lands and still came out the other end of the tunnel unsuccessful.

From inside the house, Jonah heard his father, Russell, call out. "C'mon Martha, there, there now. It'll be over real soon," tears rolled down her face. She wanted to believe in his words but knew better.

She knew it was coming, just a matter of when. Today was the day it would all come to an end. The struggles, hard times, the land, and all the debt that Russell had built up trying to survive all the rough times. It was an end of an era. Everything that they had earned, everything that they had owned, everything that they had proved themselves worthy of, was going to meet its end. *'We came from the dirt, and to dirt, we shall return,'* she thought to herself.

Moments later, his parents stepped out onto the porch and joined their son, turning their craggy, weather-beaten faces and peered at the approaching procession with saddened eyes. There could not be anything more depressing than watching one's hard work crumble down to dust. The sheer disappointment that one feels while watching it burn down to ashes, knowing fully well that you could not do anything no matter how badly you wanted to, has no match.

Jonah knew the oncoming cars and trucks were not welcome guests. There would be no birthday party today. No, no party today or maybe ever again. The thoughts swirling in his mind like an enraged tornado were now hurting his brain. He could feel it burning his heart, putting each and every vein in his body on fire.

Russell Knight was a tall gaunt man with, six-foot frame with a gray receding hairline, un-shaven face who appeared ten years older than his actual age of fifty-two. His hands dirty and callused from working the fields. He was wearing his torn, dirty denim overalls, dark plaid shirt, and boots with holes on the soles, and a dirty, flannel wool jacket.

His wife, Martha, was a slender five feet-four inches' tall woman with long salt and pepper hair rolled into a bun. She also appeared a decade older than her forty-six years. Martha always wore a long floral dress without any definition and dirty tied boots. She looked like the definition of a farm girl.

Jonah was wearing raggedy torn overalls, a plaid shirt with the sleeves rolled up, and worn old laced-up work boots. His jacket was too large for his slender young body, and the fact that it was borrowed was evident in its outlook.

Each one of them had something in common; neither one knew much of anything outside their community. All three were locally schooled in the schoolhouse at the edge of town with Mrs. Bertha Anderson, who had been teaching for the last twenty-seven years. Bertha taught all the children and a few adults all the basic courses. Reading, writing, and mathematics. She had seen generations grow up right in front of her eyes, and she knew she had taught them well. What more was there to teach anyway to kids whose fate had been sealed by the farms their families owned?

She was quite a large woman of five feet, nine inches tall, with a powerful, loud commanding voice, but always kind with a helping hand to anyone that needed special attention. Even though she had a limited amount of knowledge to impart to the kids regarding the courses they were taught at school, she made sure that she compensated for it by teaching them manners and kindness and the etiquette to live in this beautiful, beautiful world.

However, for those who tried to come in her way, she was a living hell. Nobody was to mess with her. The people in town would joke that no one would dare get into a fight with that woman. She would tear them apart;

if not by words, she would punch them into submission. Yes, Bertha Anderson was one tough lady.

"All grades," she would say, "You've got to go to school, everybody. If you do not show up, I will find you and drag you to school."

Since 1928, the year Russell Knight was granted the ten-acre land by the government. They had been able to grind out a decent living for a few years. Those people in congress always called them, 'Squatters with Rights.'

The fields that once produced the best potatoes, wheat, and corn in Hays, were the best in the state according to people and were known for their products. Now, the fertile ground had been replaced by one foot of dust. The area was as dry as a desert in the middle of nowhere.

"I can fight the land, but I can't fight God," Russell told his wife the day the foreclosure notice came from Hays National Bank. Even though the acreage came from a land grant, the Knights borrowed money to keep the farm going, using it as collateral and driving themselves into more debt.

That was the thing. He did not know his limits. He did not realize when he needed to stop, when it was time to let go. He continued on investing on a land that was bound to fail him because the Dust Bowl had no friends. It treated everyone alike and made no mistake.

Sighing, Russell stepped forward, straightened to his full six-foot frame placing his large calloused, tanned hand on his son's mussed sandy hair. "It'll be all right, Jonah, sorry, son," he muttered as the first of the sedans screeched to a stop in front of the house.

He was sorry for not passing it on as a heritage to his son. He was sorry that his practices had made him see this day – rue it. He was sorry that he did not let it go when there was still time to save himself and his family. He was sorry that he could not leave something behind for his son.

The black Ford was the first to arrive with the words "County Auctioneer" printed on the sides of the front doors. The second vehicle, a two-tone maroon and black four-door Packard, stopped behind the Ford. The caravan had finally reached its destination.

The drivers' door swung open from the Packard. A stocky man in a dark gray double-breasted pinstriped suit, black western boots, gray Stetson hat with a wide flowered necktie, and a gold tie pin climbed out.

Tyrone Rhodes was the President of the Bank and the Bank's owner. He was a short, stocky man with a round face and a large mustache that was curled at either end. His hair was neatly pasted down with pomade gel, and his pinstriped suit jacket was blowing slightly in the mild breeze. His watch fob was neatly tucked into the vest pocket.

Jonah's eyes went directly to the long dark Churchill cigar that protruded out of the corner of the man's mouth. He let out a plume of smoke and twirled his large mustache. Although he was a couple of inches shorter than Jonah's father, he seemed like a giant to the boy.

"Mornin', Mr. Rhodes," Russell Knight said.

Tyrone Rhodes nodded, plucking his gold watch from his vest. He glanced at it and announced, "Almost eight, time to start the auction," he bellowed heartily as if it was a fun thing to do, completely ignorant of the feelings of the Knight family.

"Sorry about this, folks, but like I told you and Martha, I may own the Bank, but it's not my money. All I do is keep an eye on it for the depositors and investors. Sorry folks, but business is business," he said in a robotic voice, a voice that was completely devoid of emotion.

By this time, Jonah's eyes widened when he saw the procession of more than a dozen cars and trucks rambling down the road lining up in front of the house and down the gravel road. The dust was rising into clouds of dirt. The clouds that he knew would stay in the skies for longer than they were supposed to.

They were filled with neighbors and strangers from the nearby towns. He recognized some as the parents of his schoolmates. The murmurings from the throng buzzed through the air like a swarm of wasps. Some called out to the Knights in sympathy.

"We know that you did your best but we're all having hard times now."

"God bless you, Martha, stay strong," some of the women would say.

"So sorry! We are here for you," Shaking their heads from side to side.

Russell wiped his brow with a red checkered handkerchief from around his neck and gave a resigning nod. Jonah maintained his eyes on Rhodes. He did not like him; in fact, not too many people liked him. He was all business. There was something about him that Jonah certainly did not like and which made him uncomfortable as well. His stare was almost piercing Jonah's entire body.

Rhodes then turned to the man still seated behind the wheel of the County Auctioneer's car. "Let's go, Pete. We got an auction to conduct here," he said with a snicker twisting his mustache – no doubt he was enjoying the misery of the people.

The door of the Ford swung open, a husky, long-limbed, tall man wearing black alligator cowboy boots and a wide-brimmed brown Stetson, squarely planted solidly on his head, a solid 3-piece black suit, white shirt, and a narrow polo black tie with a silver and gold clip stepped out.

Peter Flagstaff, the County Auctioneer, was a burly man standing six foot one inch, with his belly pushing slightly out over his pants, which were held up by thick three-inch-wide blue and white striped suspenders.

Rhodes turned to the Knights and jerked his thumb at the Auctioneer. "You all know Pete Flagstaff; he's a fair and square man." Russell and Martha again nodded grimly. Everyone knew what fair and square meant when it came from the mouth of Rhodes.

When Peter Flagstaff brushed by Jonah, he reached out with his hand to the young man's head and mussed his hair. Jonah flicked his eyes at the man and turned away, feeling like he was just stepped on, but he could not take his eyes off him.

Jonah was fascinated by this large stature man. There was something about him that would not let him take his eyes off the County Auctioneer. Jonah was transfixed by every move that he made, how he walked, and most of all, how he took total charge of everything.

"I suggest you all stay in the house while Pete conducts his business," Rhodes said. "When we get to the house, you gotta wait outside, OK? It'll be easier for everyone concerned," Rhodes ordered the audience, and everyone agreed.

"Let's go, Pete; we got an auction to run," Rhodes said again, "Let's go," Rhodes commanded.

Jonah tugged at his father's patched, worn shirtsleeve. "Pa, you tell me, please, what's goin' on? Are they goin' to take me away?"

Russell and his wife exchanged glances. "Let's just go inside, boy." Inside the house, the Knights huddled, sitting around the kitchen table. Not a word was spoken as they sat in total silence.

Over the next two and a half hours, Flagstaff bellowed the words loudly, "SOLD," repeatedly. The Knights did not speak, just stared at one another. They listened, hearing all their possessions being sold off for pennies on the dollar – the tractor, the hand plow, livestock, truck, shovels, tool shed, the corals for the livestock, and all the remaining assets in the barn and everything outside.

When finally, Flagstaff worked his way to the house. He announced loudly, "OK folks, it's now time for the furniture and all the rest of the stuff in the house, so ladies, keep a sharp eye out. Folks, gotta ask you to step outside, please," he said softly.

"Come on Russell, get the family outside. We gotta sell the house furniture and other stuff," Rhodes said almost as a command.

Without a word, the three walked out of the house and sat on the porch swing as the people walked in to buy whatever they could.

Martha Knight clung to her husband and wept as Russel patted her gently on her back. "Easy woman, it'll soon be over. I'm sorry, Martha, really I tried to make it work, we tried..." he trailed off as tears ran down his face.

Jonah felt his throat tighten and his blue eyes well up, but no tears came out. Not now, he said to himself. This will never happen to me, NEVER! He thought. Jonah never had such determination and focus. It appeared he became cold and disconcerting about the whole situation. He was just a child! No child should ever have to go through what he was going through at this young age.

What appeared to be moments later, the auction started anew in the house, and for the next hour and a half, the word "SOLD!" echoed throughout the house repeatedly. Everything was sold – furniture, lamps, pots and pans, dishes, even the sagging tasseled red velvet sofa with two broken springs in the middle.

In the end, Flagstaff gathered everybody outside to sell the property. Jonah watched with absolute fascination. Every move that Flagstaff did not miss. Everything that he said as he watched how he had control of everything.

When the un-merciful auction ended, Tyrone Rhodes strode outside and told Russell to come into the house. He reached into his pocket and brought out a big roll of fives, tens and twenties, and a few fifty-dollar bills. The banker peeled off two twenties, three-five, and six single dollar bills and handed it to Russell Knight. "Sixty-one dollars for you to get a new start there, Russell," he said as if he did him a huge favor by selling everything he owned for pennies.

"That's what's left. I threw in a few dollars more for you," the banker said arrogantly. "You can stay on for a few more days, but that's all. Then you gotta get out, OK?"

Not waiting for an answer, Rhodes turned and walked quickly, got into his large Packard, drove it in a circle, and promptly raced down the gravel road raising the dirt behind him. Peter Flagstaff said, "Sorry folks, but that is the way it goes. Can't help ya." He strolled to his car and drove off with the rest of the crowd rambling back down the gravel road.

That evening after finishing supper, a bowl of chicken soup, and a couple of slices of three-day-old bread, Russell Knight pushed back from the table and shuffled out of the kitchen, stopping to look at his family with sad eyes. Those were the eyes of a man who had failed to provide for his family. The guilt was eating him from the inside. Tonight was going to be a tough night, but if he waited it out, there might just be another hope with the dawn. All he needed to do was survive tonight, and he would come out of it alive. But the thoughts… the thoughts were killing him a little with each passing minute. *'What to do of the mind that never rests?'* he asked himself silently.

"Russell, where ya goin'? Martha asked. Gotta go to the barn for a bit," he responded. He paused for a moment, staring at the two sitting at the table. "Love you both," he said as he walked out the door. Why did that *'love you'* sound like a goodbye?

"It'll be over soon, I promise," Russel said as he headed out the door.

A few minutes later, the roar of a pistol blast echoed from the barn, breaking the quiet stillness of the early evening.

Startled by the noise, they both ran out the door racing to the barn. When young Jonah and his mother opened the large barn door, they found Russell Knight dead in one of the stalls. Next to him laid the Remington revolver. His body, motionless as the blood ran out of his head from the gunshot. *All he needed was to survive the night...!*

Martha fell to her knees next to her husband, sobbing uncontrollably. A dry-eyed Jonah just stared like a stone sculpture, frozen in time. He could not shed a tear, just stared at his father laying there, dead. The distant coldness from the morning had returned to his eyes.

The next morning after a sleepless night, Jonah arose and rubbed his eyes with his knuckles. When he peered out from his bedroom window, his jaw fell open, gasping for air. Martha was swinging from the old oak tree in the front yard. She had used the rope from the tree's tire swing.

Everything had finally come to an end. Her life was over the same as Russel's. She could no longer deal with the thought of losing everything, including the only man she had ever known and loved and cherished. She could not deal with not being the farm girl. And in their selfish need to get away from the failure, they had abandoned their son, leaving him alone to his devices in this big bad world after he had just lost everything.

As with his father, Jonah Knight stood immobile as he watched his mother's lifeless body slowly swing in the morning air. The creaking of the tree's limb mingled with the sounds and caws of the circling crows, ready to gnaw at her dead flesh.

Jonah Knight couldn't shed a tear as a quieting numbness overcame him. He just stared out the window, looking at everything, but seeing nothing, just a blank,

cold stare.

2.

CHAPTER TWO

The following day after a sleepless night, he packed everything he owned and wrapped it up in an old torn bed sheet, tied it together using the ends, threw it across his shoulder and walked down the dusty gravel road toward the main highway never looking back at the house, just looking forward with a mission on his mind.

Martha took the auction money that Rhodes gave to Russell and put it into her pocket. She had hidden it in one of Jonah's socks for later. But that later was not going to come, was it? She had made it clear by taking her own life. Both of them, in their minute of desperation, had chosen themselves, not once thinking about Jonah and what he would do once they are gone. *Selfish. The whole lot of 'em.*

Once he reached the road, he stuck out his thumb trying to hitchhike a ride to town. He had made up his mind. He was not going to stay and take pity from the whole town. His parents had chosen what they had chosen for themselves, it was time for him to choose now. And he had chosen himself.

About ten minutes later, a car showed up in the distant horizon. Jonah's hopes got better of him. After what it seemed like ages of waiting, someone had finally showed up. It was a neighbor driving his rickety old '32 black Ford pickup truck, who stopped when he saw a kid hitchhiking in the middle of the gravel road.

"Hey, kid, where ya goin?" The neighbor asked. "Hey, aren't you the Knight kid?" he recognized Jonah from the auction.

"I'm goin' to town, sir. Could you give me a ride? I'll sit in the back if you want," was his reply. Short and precise!

"That's ok, boy; you can sit up here with me. Sorry to hear about your Paw, real sad, shame, sorry boy. What happened to your Ma? Where is she?" the neighbor asked upon realizing that the kid was alone right after his father had just died. *Unusual...!*

"Gotta tell the Sheriff that she hung herself from the old oak out back," Jonah replied coldly.

It did not look like he had just lost both of his parents and his property in a matter of two days. He had grown cold and distant from the world. His eyes looked like ice blue Ocean, dangerous, deep and threatening, but cold. The blue orbs showed no mercy or emotion, neither for his parents nor for anyone paying him condolences over their untimely departure.

The trip was silent with the exception to the loud noise of the gravel hitting the front and back fenders of the truck as it sped along the road with a cloud of dry dust kicking up in the rear as they headed toward town.

His heart had grown hard and detached from everything and everyone. Nothing had affected him in the past forty-eight hours. Like the dirt that had turned against its inhabitants, he had closed the walls of his heart on the world as well. What awaited him was a ruthless life that he was ready to lead.

'Thank you kindly, sir," Jonah replied getting out of the truck in front of the local *Feed and Tack* store which was only a few doors down from the Sheriff's office.

"Sure thing, kid, don't forget to grab your stuff and eat something, take this quarter and eat, OK?" the neighbor gave him a quarter to buy some food.

Jonah walked down to tell the sheriff what happened.

"I would appreciate it if you can take care of the matters from now onwards. *From details to their bodies.*" He ended his narration of the event with this. Following an in-depth explanation of what he saw, Jonah still could not shed a tear or even a sign of remorse. There certainly was no love in the Knight house. And a loveless marriage can only give birth to a loveless child – a cold and distant boy who was unable to cry even at the death of his parents.

"What can I do for you, boy? You can stay at a few places in town if you want," was the Sheriff's reply. Jonah couldn't figure out whether it was out of pity or he genuinely cared about him.

"Thank you, sir," Jonah replied. "I think that I'll find my way," he said as he started to walk out the front door without contemplating on the offer for a second. Jonah wanted no favors from anybody because he thought that he would have to pay it back like a loan.

"Take this fifty-cent piece boy," he said as he flipped the coin, "Get yourself something to eat," he said. "Go to the coffee shop and tell the waitress that

Sherriff Jake sent you. She'll take care of you," Sheriff tried to console him in his own way.

Jonah had some very troubling thoughts and remained very much focused on his journey. The thoughts were burning his insides, churning his mind. The image of his mother hanging from the Oak tree was still there right behind his eyelids; he couldn't shake it off no matter how hard he tried to. It didn't affect him emotionally, but it was there.

Then there was the sheer humiliation that he and his family had faced the other day. The humiliation that had taken the life of his parents – the auction. He had never thought that it would come down to this someday, but it had. All that mattered now was how he dealt with it. And that was his next journey. *'Dealing with it was exactly what he would do,'* he thought to himself with utter determination.

He had a burning desire to seek out and find the County Auctioneer, Peter Flagstaff. He was on a mission that was of great importance, he had to, and he must find him. Only Flagstaff could help him achieve the goal he had sworn upon. The goal he left his home to search for.

The look on Jonah's face was like that of a hunter preparing to search for his prey. His determination became stronger and more intense. *'I must find him, no matter what,'* he thought to himself as rage burned through his body.

As Jonah walked through the town, people extended sympathy with a look of sadness, but all he could do was to say, "Thank you kindly."

Jonah was always taught to be a gentleman. None of that foul language the other boys would use ever got to him. To be courteous and respectful was what he was taught by his parents, "Always be a gentleman," his Mother instilled in him since he was a little boy.

He was very much focused, not allowing anything to be distracting. He was looking for Flagstaff. *'I need to talk to Mister Flagstaff. I must talk to him,'* he thought to himself. Flagstaff was the only thing on his mind; his eyes were scouring everything, in every direction. He investigated every store quickly and left to continue his journey. His anxiety was building up immensely.

He did not want to be anything like his parents. He hated the way things were, and in retrospect, he hated his parents. Jonah was determined to make something of himself. Be somebody who everyone respected and looked up to. He promised himself that he would be nothing like his parents, ever.

There was no love between Martha & Russell in the house, no hugging, and no one to ever say *'I love you'* or tuck you into bed. He felt emotionally unstable but tried to stay grounded. He mostly stayed to himself and didn't talk too much even when his parents were alive. Now he had all the more reason. People did not expect him to say much as they thought he would be grieving.

Someday he would find someone to share his life with. But that day was far away from today. First, he was trying to make something of himself. *'And maybe, just maybe, Flagstaff... yes, yes, he was the answer,'* his mind raced.

Jonah started walking faster, up to one side of the street and down the other and stopping only to investigate, gazing into every store, looking for him. His pulse started to race faster, holding tightly to his tied-up bed sheet with all that he owned. He had to find him. Jonah started to run as if someone was chasing him; he ran faster, breaking into a sweat.

He had to find him. With this sense of urgency, his stomach started to churn with nervousness and hunger. *'Where are you,'* he thought, *'Where are you, Mr. Flagstaff? Please be here; where are you?'*

Finally, exhausted, turning the last corner on Mead Street, Jonah saw him sitting outside of Oliver's, the local Tavern, with a beer in hand, laughing with a few of the other men. They talked about the funny things that take place at the auctions and the good buys that some of them received at the Knight Farm auction.

3.

CHAPTER THREE

Jonah stopped, frozen in his tracks feeling as though he just stepped into a puddle of thick cement.

What does he say to such an important man? He stared at him at a distance for a few minutes which seemed to be hours, wanting to talk to him, in his mind so many questions were running at once, he thought.

Jonah had no fears, especially from other people, but Flagstaff scared him. He was such a large, domineering force when he was around, people became nervous, and a bit threatened. How should I talk to him, or approach him, or should I just stand here? What should I do? He questioned himself.

Finally, after a few minutes what seemed to be hours, he walked closer until he was ten feet away, stopped, and just stared at him. *Unable to decide what to do.*

After a few moments, Flagstaff noticed him, asking, "What's wrong, boy? What do ya want?" it took Jonah by surprise, yet he was still unable to formulate a sentence to speak. Maybe, Flagstaff realized it. "Come on boy, speak up, don't be shy, I won't bite. What's your name, boy?" he said with his deep baritone voice. He didn't even remember who Jonah was or that he sold everything that his parents owned and destroyed the only world that he knew.

"Speak up now or move along," Flagstaff said with a demanding voice.

After a few moments, nervously, Jonah answered,

"My name is Jonah Knight, Sir; you sold my parent's farm and everything we owned. Just last week, you sold it clean through."

"Did a good job, didn't I?" he joked with a smile. "Hell, of a sale wasn't it," as he snickered.

"So, what do you want boy?" Flagstaff asked.

After a moment of silence, Jonah said, "Will you teach me?"

"Whatcha talking about, boy," "Teach you what?" Flagstaff blurted out with a gruff deep voice.

"I want to become like you," Jonah said nervously.

"What the hell are you talking about? Better explain yourself, boy?" Flagstaff said with a nervous laugh.

"I want to learn how to be an Auctioneer," was Jonah's reply.

"Be a farmer, storekeeper, or something else, boy, now go away, gotta finish my beer," Flagstaff said, turning his chair inward.

Jonah didn't flinch as he held his ground firmly as if his feet were set in freshly poured concrete. He knew it was now or never, and how dare a man who ended the world for him with his work tell him to become someone else. *To choose some other work.*

He just stared at him coldly and said more firmly, raising his voice slightly elevated.

"Will you teach me?"

"I'm not going anywhere, sir, until you agree to teach me," Jonah said. "Teach you what, boy, what do you really want?" said Flagstaff.

Starting to bargain with Flagstaff, Jonah said, "I'll work for you for nothing.' Mornin to dark if you'll teach me."

"Again, I'll ask you again, teach you what, boy?" Jonah was unable to make sense of this question. Had

Flagstaff not heard him the first time, or is he just acting naïve? While he was contemplating, Flagstaff spoke again, "Come on, come on, speak up and talk to me boy, talk to me!" Flagstaff said firmly. "Ya gotta go the school and learn something, not me!" He exclaimed.

Jonah said with a firm voice as he could for a boy of eight and a half years. Since he was more mature beyond his years, man, but pleasant to listen to. "I want to become an Auctioneer like you", Jonah replied.

"What!" Flagstaff said with a surprised voice. Why do you want to become an Auctioneer? Give me one good reason, boy and then I'll think about it. Just give me one good reason," he said laughingly.

"Because you just do your job and get paid for it. People respect and kinda fear you, Mr. Flagstaff, I've got nothing and no one and I'm hungry. I gotta make somthin' of myself," Jonah replied as he clutched his pole holding the bundle tightly with both hands.

"Please, Mr. Flagstaff, will you teach me? I ain't got nothin else and nothin to lose."

"Go on, kid, get the hell out of here and don't bother me and leave me alone," Flagstaff insisted.

He turned toward the other men at the table and continued to join the conversation. Jonah did not move, standing silently.

"I said get out of here and let me alone, now scram kid," Flagstaff said abruptly.

After a few moments, Jonah turned away with his head lowered. Turning back, facing Flagstaff with determination, silently saying to himself, "I will be back tomorrow, yes, tomorrow. I will win," he thought to himself with fierce determination.

Since it was late in the afternoon and nowhere to go, he walked behind the bar and found a quiet place on the side of the garbage cans to sleep for the night. Not wanting to return to the farm which he hated, besides what else did the farm had to offer to him. Nothing but horrible thoughts of the last two days. *His very own*

gravel road nightmare.

4.

CHAPTER FOUR

The following morning, Clyde Blake, the owner of the bar was throwing out the trash from the night before. Clyde found him sleeping by the cans in the rear of the building, woke him, and brought Jonah into the bar.

Told him to wash up and then fed him some breakfast. Clyde told him that he could stay here if he worked for it.

Jonah agreed to this as he was giving something to Clyde back, instead of just getting advantages that he would be asked to return some day if he didn't provide his services today. Jonah scrubbed the floor, cleaned the bathrooms, the bar, washed glasses and dishes, and general cleaning.

As the days and months passed quickly, Jonah was confident in himself. From days of not doing anything, to the days where he can be assistance of manual labor gave him a surge of confidence in his abilities.

It was a hot Tuesday afternoon, as Jonah walked around the town just to see it. *WOW!* He thought. This is beautiful. He never thought that the town was so large. When he returned to the bar, Flagstaff walked in sweating, demanding a cold beer.

Jonah thought that maybe this will be the day. As he walked back to the bar and to his astonishment, there he was, the man he felt was going to be his future, *Peter Flagstaff.*

Proudly Jonah walked up to him and with a demanding voice, "Mr. Flagstaff, I can be a great help to you. I can clean house and even cook a bit. You need me because you're a lonely man living alone and I'm good company. Please, sir, please!" he said and tried to touch him where it hurts the most by reminding Flagstaff of the only thing he lacked. *Companionship.*

"Mr. Flagstaff, will you teach me? He said softly."

Flagstaff was no kid at this game, he stared at him carefully for a few minutes, finally saying, "OK, kid, listen to me and listen to me good. I'll put it to you this way, I live alone, and I like it. I sure don't want a messy kid asking me question after question. I'm not a teacher and I don't want company, so get off me. Got it!"

Persistently, Jonah continued to push the issue further. Finally relenting, admiring his stamina and determination, Flagstaff starred at the boy.

"Listen, kid, I'll teach you under one condition." "You do not ever question me on what I do, only how I do it. Can you keep your mouth shut and your eyes and ears open, boy? You gotta listen to what I say and nothing more."

"Yes sir, yes sir. Can I stay at your house? I promise I won't be any trouble. I can stay in the barn if you like. I'll do all of the chores if you like and take care of your family," Jonah said anxiously. He rambled on and on without catching his breath. He was very eager to move out of the bar, trying to keep his excited emotions contained but evidently failing to do so. After all, he had only seen eight birthdays of his life, he was still a kid.

"No family, boy, just me," Flagstaff replied. Jonah knew that he lived alone, he was just testing, using caution.

"Nope, you can live in the house, I don't have a barn. Are you clean, I can't stand a messy or smelly, dirty kid ya know? You gotta wash every day. Don't want a stinking kid around. Can you do it, boy?" Flagstaff said.

"How ya doin, Pete?" as two men walked in the bar and sat beside Flagstaff, while hearing the conditions he kept in front of the boy. After the conversation, the other two men started to snicker,

"Pete, are ya really gonna do it? You gotta cleaning lady already."

"Yep, why not, I can use the company for a change."

"By the way, what did you say your name was? I can't keep calling you boy," Flagstaff asked.

"Jonah, Jonah, Jonah Knight, sir. Yes, sir, I can do that, I mean, I'm a clean person." Jonah said excitedly. "Smart too," he added. "I learn stuff real fast." He made sure that he forms best of his impression.

"How old are you kid?"

"Eight and a half sir, just turned, but I'm smart and act older sir," Jonah replied or reminded him again of how good of a decision Flagstaff made.

5.

CHAPTER FIVE

Peter Flagstaff lived in a large house at the north edge of the town at the end of Gopher Street. He never married, never found the right lady so he was looking forward to having some company and someone to talk to after so many years of being alone.

The house was too large for just one person. It had two stories with balconies circling around the entire first, and second levels. Each side with white wicker tables, chairs and a bench on either side that were tied down so that nothing would blow away during the high winds. The house was painted blue with white trim on the exterior. Blue in any shade was ok since it was his favorite color. It reminded him of the ocean that he saw in his various travels and was very calming to the eye. Just like Jonah's eyes. *Not big of a coincidence.*

Surrounding the house was an array of bright flowers and bushes set in rows touching the steps leading up to the front porch. Flower boxes were under each of the first-floor windows, which the housekeeper monitored and watered daily. She planted daisies and other colorful flowers.

All the rooms of the house were large, with an average size kitchen which was big enough for a six-foot table in the middle of the room. He didn't cook for himself, except for the morning coffee, sandwiches, and light snacks that were easy to make.

Surprisingly though, there were two bathrooms, one on each floor. Each bathroom had a bathtub and a showerhead. The toilets were water closets and had water tanks on the top.

There were a few oil lamps in the living room on the white linen-covered tables. There was a very unusually large antique lamp over the hand-carved walnut mantle over the fireplace, just in case the electricity went out as it normally did when the winds blew harshly across the plains.

Outside there were storm shutters on all the windows outside and doors to protect from the high, strong winds.

Frilly curtains were on all the windows with curved shades to block the sunlight. There was a large, curved walnut desk in the corner of the living room, angled facing the front door, which he used for an office, with two wooden file cabinets behind it and two large oak, and matching six-shelf bookcases. There were three wooden chairs in front of the desk. His chair was an overstuffed maroon wingback leather swivel chair that was built especially for him placed in the center behind the desk.

He did not invite people over unless they were people that he did business with. He was a very private person indeed.

The house was always kept clean by Mrs. Johannessen, the housekeeper who came in once a week to clean and three days a week to cook for him whenever he was in town.

The basement had some canned food, three bunk beds with blankets in case the tornados came across the weather-torn area. It felt like Flagstaff kept himself prepared for every kind of natural catastrophe.

There was one room in the basement that Jonah was forbidden to enter located in the west corner of the dimly lit section, no matter what. This mysterious concrete-lined walled room was held closed with two large, firm locks attached to a solid steel door.

Since he was one of the few Auctioneers within the five surrounding territories, he was able to obtain all the furniture and accessories he needed to furnish his house. Obviously, it was an eclectic display of oddities,

as one would find anywhere.

6.

CHAPTER SIX

The years passed quickly; Flagstaff took Jonah under his wing, bought him new clothes, fed him, and took care of him as best he could. He treated him as if he was his own. After all, he had no one else, and it felt good to take care of someone. He was satisfying his innate human tendency of nurturing.

As promised, Jonah was very careful never to ask too many questions unless it had to do with the business of Auctioneering.

Peter Flagstaff also kept his promise and taught him almost everything he knew about an Auctioneer's life and how to run the business. He was overly cautious and guarded not to tell him about his other secret life, abilities, and travels. He taught him how to talk to people, what to ask, what not to ask, what to say and how to say it.

"Be a good listener," he constantly impressed upon him. He told him that numbers are the most important things when selling at an auction.

"Always remember that what you are looking for is generally in clear plain sight. You just have to look harder to find it," Flagstaff always told him.

Peter Flagstaff was certainly very secretive about certain things. He would take trips for two or three weeks at a time, leaving Jonah under the supervision of the housekeeper.

He would always leave either early in the morning or late in the night. He would return without saying a word.

This would repeat ever so often, but this time Jonah thought he will inquire about the missing of Flagstaff.

When Flagstaff came back, to leave once again. Jonah took the opportunity to satiate his quest. He tried to ask, only to receive a short yet sharp answer, "Hey, I told you don't ask, don't you ever ask me about my trips, got it?" he reminded him of the pact they made at the bar. He continued with a stern voice.

"Just listen to what I tell you, *OK?* Do you understand me, boy? Mind your own fuckin' damn business, boy."

"Yes, Sir, never again. Sorry Mr. Flagstaff, I mean Sir." Jonah said in fear that he might get thrown out of the house, never to be taught again.

"Call me Pete or Peter, not Mr. Flagstaff, got it?" He turned and headed up the stairs angrily, stomping on each stair. Making sure that his words were not just heard but must be remembered by heart.

Something weighed heavily on Flagstaff's mind today; he wondered if he made the right decision by bringing Jonah into his secretive, mysterious, and very dangerous life.

He must never be found out, he thought to himself. This is too dangerous for his life, gotta protect him, he thought to himself, gotta protect this boy. He was puzzled by his feelings towards Jonah. This was new to him. *Taking care of something other than his own needs? Never happened before!*

7.

CHAPTER SEVEN

Jonah worked side by side with him, doing house chores or whatever it took for him to learn the business, absorbing everything like a giant sea sponge.

He grew into a tall, fine young man, standing five foot, eleven inches, lean stature, and very handsome figure and always a gentleman.

Flagstaff would say, "Jonah, you gotta think on your feet and be fast, always, look around you, note everything that is taking place, and most of all, be very, very careful," careful of what, he thought.

Over the years, several times during the summer and winter months, Flagstaff would take Jonah out into the plains and teach him how to shoot his vast array of guns, rifles, and shotguns. He even taught him how to handle a knife just in case a gun wasn't available. He made sure that Jonah knew how to protect himself in every case.

"Whatever you do, Son, be a good shot. Never miss your target, *NEVER*," he shouted, "Got it? Sometimes you only have one chance, and it might save your life someday," Flagstaff kept telling him.

Peter Flagstaff was raised and educated in Springfield, Illinois, where he received a degree from the Springfield City Community College. He moved to Hays in June of 1930 to seek and establish a business career. He felt that it would be easier to make more money if he were in a smaller town, without any competition for his very secretive and specialized skills. He would hide in plain sight, trying to be low key which was nearly impossible.

Flagstaff taught Jonah how to speak proper English, "no slang," he would say, learn and understand mathematics, history, geography, and bookkeeping methods. He also made sure that Jonah remembered everything, constantly testing him every night over dinner.

From taking a boy in only to teach him what he asked for to teaching him things necessary for surviving as the fittest option, something transitioned in Flagstaff, and it showed.

This was a skill that was necessary for the art of negotiating or selling with anybody. Peter Flagstaff enrolled Jonah at the University of Chicago to make sure that he was well educated. He graduated in just a few short years with an excellent general education. He knew geography, English, and a bit of a few languages.

"Always remember the facts," Flagstaff would say. "Never forget and be a good listener. People will tell you anything that they know as long as there is someone to listen to them." He said, for him, it might be just one of the laws of auctioneering, but in his business, Flagstaff cracked the code of human relations.

"Look around you at all times and remember that whatever you are looking for is hidden in plain sight. Just look a bit harder."

Jonah absorbed everything like a large empty hole looking to be filled. He listened in silence every time Flagstaff talked, always paying attention to detail, and his mind never wandered off elsewhere.

Over the next several years, Flagstaff's health slowly deteriorated, his body now riddled with arthritis, problems with his lungs, coughing most of the time from the winds that carried the ground dust from the open prairie. His mysterious travels slowed down, and he did not go out much.

He moved his bedroom down to the main level of the house since the stairs became a challenge to climb. Being overweight did not help him either. Jonah looked up to and admired him like a father figure. Even though Jonah had a family before, this was the closest he came to live the feeling of family. They spent time making it a point to talk to each other every evening over dinner.

Finally, two years later, Flagstaff, while over dinner, said, "Jonah, it's the time!"

"Time for what?" he replied with a surprised look.

"I'm not feeling all that good, and I just can't do it anymore. You've noticed that I can't walk very well. I think that you're ready." He confessed and said, "Are you ready, Jonah? I've taught you all I can, and I turned a boy into a man," Flagstaff said as he continued, "You must keep me informed on what you are doing at all times. Is that okay?" Jonah stared at him for a few moments and, with a sense of deep sadness, "agreed."

"I talked to my clients and told them that you're going to take over, including that old Son of a Bitch, Rhodes at the bank." He continued, "Always hated that

Bastard, but he made me a lot of money. I also told a particularly good friend of mine about you. They might contact you for a, umm, special job. You can trust him, but always be careful." He said with care evident in his eyes. His eyes were not any more of a cold-hearted Auctioneer Jonah met in the past. "Ya never know who might want to kill you."

"Always remember that some or most of the things that you might be looking for are usually hidden in plain sight. Repeated it, didn't I? Keep your eyes sharp and open all the time. If you are not careful and expect the unexpected, that will save your life or kill you," Flagstaff told him.

"Been doing this for a long time Jonah, fourteen years is enough training for you, and besides, I'm sick and tired of looking at your ugly face," he said with a smile. *Ah, Flagstaff and his choices of words!* "You're on your own now. Always remember what I taught you, okay? Always stay sharp and be alert. Watch your back, remember that at all times, watch your back, got it, boy?"

Flagstaff died in the winter of 1960, leaving everything that he had to Jonah.

There was property and all the money he had saved over the years, one hundred, twenty-three thousand dollars in cash, and a place that never became 'home' for him worth almost seventeen thousand more. There were mementoes, trophies, gold, silver, and everything else that this man had collected over the span of forty-eight years. Peter Flagstaff was only 67 years old, and yet his collection of goods were more or less around the golden treasure of Ali Baba, which was collected for millions of years.

Jonah Knight stayed on in the house. He used it as his home and office, where he greeted new clients and negotiated some exceptional deals. Jonah kept in mind all the details that he was cautioned not to forget and became the Auctioneer of everybody's choice. He was very sharp and cunning, always remembering and honoring eyes on facts. That is what Flagstaff taught him.

Mrs. Johannessen stayed on as long as she could, but her age and time caught up with her. She couldn't work anymore, and he had to find a replacement.

8.

CHAPTER EIGHT

One year later, at twenty-three, Jonah was known by everyone in the tri-state area for being tough and meticulous in his work. At this young age, people respected him and called him Sir, or Mr. Knight, as he walked around town. The local people would always make it a point to acknowledge him.

"Morning, Jonah," they would yell from across the street. It almost appeared like they were in fear of him thinking that their property might be sold, and they all wanted to be his friend. In fear of getting on his bad side, they made sure that they were forever on his good side.

When he traveled to other local cities, Jonah would demand only the best accommodations in the best hotels. Several of the local banks would call upon him for his expertise, even for the most minor issues. Jonah always charged a fee for his consulting services, no matter how small of a deal it was for him.

Annually, Jonah would attend The National Auctioneers Conference held at McCormack place convention hall in Chicago and stay at the Palmer House on State Street.

This year he was attending the convention; he was standing at the bar in the hotel having a nice cold beer, staring at the opening, facing the main entrance when seven men walked through the lobby. It appears the one main person was surrounded by an entire entourage with him.

Jonah walked into the lobby to get a closer look at the new arrivals. He leaned up against the wall and watched.

One of the men was especially noticeable. He was surrounded by the other men to protect him. He looked like he was around Jonah's age. They had paused in the middle of the room, talking while one man went up to the desk to inquire about the best accommodations.

Hearing a slight noise from the ceiling, Jonah looked up to the newly installed large stained-glass chandelier on the ceiling. It started to loosen at the connection it had with the roof. The bolts were not holding; they fell on the hand-woven carpet in the lobby. Nobody seemed to notice the fixture pulling away from the ceiling. Jonah watched as it continued to loosen. Now, it was only held by the electrical wire that gave it power. Jonah watched as it slowly slipped. He knew what would be happening next if he didn't move in time.

Immediately, he sprints into action and ran toward the group of men standing directly under its path of sure death to anyone under it. As he lunged toward the men, pushing them away and down on the floor. The fixture crashed on the carpeted floor shattering the stained glass, scattering it around the room. He had pushed all men in the center who were directly under the fixture several feet away from the oncoming disaster.

As they rose up from the floor, the men stared at him with a scared sigh of relief. They immediately rushed to help one man before making sure of their own safety, enabling him to stand, brushing off the glass that remained on his clothing.

"Are you alright, my Prince? Are you hurt? Do you need anything, my Prince? My Prince, I should have protected you. I'm sorry, please forgive me." The concern turned into a compensatory tone in a matter of few portions of seconds.

All the while, Jonah watched this interaction. He must really be something for all the attention, he thought to himself.

Finally, with all the attention, the main man walked over to Jonah, who had just picked himself off the floor, brushing off the shattered glass.

"I wish to extend my thank you for saving my life. What is your name, if I may ask?"

Jonah stuttered for a minute before answering, maybe because of all attention or simply for being thanked for something. "Jonah Knight, but you can call me Jonah," he made sure to protect his identity.

"Where are you from, May I ask?" the Prince asked.

"A little town called Hays in the state of Kansas," Jonah replied.

"Mr. Jonah, I owe you my life, and I shall never forget your bravery. Your name is familiar to me. My Father mentioned you in conversation. Mr. Jonah. Thank you again. We will meet in the future, I'm sure," he said as he hurriedly walked away with his group, heading to the elevator.

The Prince whispered to one man who lingered behind and remained in the lobby talking to the desk manager. Jonah noticed a small camera being taken out of this man's pocket, taking a picture of him.

Jonah was very perplexed and puzzled. How this guy knew my name, he thought to himself.

9.

CHAPTER NINE

The following year, while he was in the process of selling the assets a small business in Otis, Kansas, just the other side of Smoky Hill, a four-hour drive south, when a stranger in the rear of the crowd kept staring and watching Jonah, his every move. That same man was watching me yesterday, and I saw him last week, Jonah thought.

He appeared like someone somewhere from the Middle East or one of the countries around there. He was thin in structure, about five foot, eight or nine inches tall, with a dark complexion wearing a wrinkled black suit, black curly hair with a wrinkled white shirt and loose tie, badly in need of a month-old shave, and his face was heavily weathered worn. His black shoes were dirty from walking through the dusty, unpaved street.

When the auction was over and the paperwork completed, he noticed that the man was still there, watching from the edge of the crowd. Jonah heard that someone was asking a lot of questions about him, which was quite irritating.

When everything was over, Jonah started to walk toward him, turned away for a moment to answer a question from one of the Buyers. When he turned back, the stranger had vanished. He was very perplexed at this, but his curiosity was peaked. He looked for him through the crowd of rambling people, but he was nowhere in sight, so he returned.

Several days later, back in Hays, while walking over to Margie's Café in the center of Main Street to get a fresh cup of her delicious coffee, the same man suddenly appeared in front of him, jolting him to a sudden stop.

"May we have a few moments to talk, sir?" the stranger asked.

"Can I help you? Do I know you?" It took few seconds for Jonah to recognize the man. "Hey, you are the guy asking questions about me? Who the hell are you?" Jonah continued questioning, speaking angrily and abruptly without giving him a chance to speak.

"Please, Mr. Knight, if you will only give me 10 minutes of your time. That's all I ask. If you do not like what I have to say, I'll leave, and you'll never see me again, please, Mr. Knight," the stranger asked, almost pleading with him seeing his rage. He agreed to listen, but for no more than the ten minutes allotted.

As they walked over to a table outside the Café, "Sit down, this is the best coffee in town," Jonah quipped.

He placed himself with his back to the outside wall of the café to make sure that there would be no one behind him.

As they sat down, Jonah started to speak, "Who," when he was abruptly interrupted,

"My name is Abdul Bomani, a servant to my Prince, umm, excuse me, my employer. You are very well known by him for your reputation. You did something for him last year, and my Prince never forgets. You were exceptionally well recommended, I might add. Your reputation goes much further than you think.

My employer watched you for quite some time and told me to speak to you personally regarding possible work. A job, if I may add. He noted your reputation of being firm with fairness by sources known only to him and may add to some extremely high circles. My Prince informed me that you are the person we have been looking for. You are Mr. Knight, Mr. Jonah

Knight?" he asked to make sure of something. "I must be sure before we continue. He told me that he is in debt to you."

Jonah paused for a few moments. Is this the guy from the hotel? Jonah himself was skeptical as to whether he should let himself be known or not. Therefore, he replied, "Maybe," Jonah asked more relaxed, "Tell me what you want," but he was guarded.

"You are Jonah Knight, yes? I have your picture here in my pocket, Mr. Knight."

At that moment, the waitress came over with her usual complimentary smile.

"Afternoon Jonah, how about a hot tuna fish with cheese or the roast beef? It is delicious today; the roast beef!"

"No thanks, Dottie, only coffee today and give me a piece of that apple pie and warm it up, will you? Thanks." After listening to Jonah's order, she moved towards the other person sitting at the table.

"And you, sir?" Abdul ordered, "Tea please, two bags, thank you." After placing the order and making sure the waitress was far away to listen, they brought back the conversation to the topic of concern.

"Now that we have settled who you are, Mr. Knight, I would like to purchase your services, to perform, a rather, err, umm, let us say, an extraordinary auction. My employer has instructed me to speak only to you. He has been looking at only you for doing this work," he continued. "We have established that you are Knight, aren't you?" Abdul asked again as Jonah didn't answer his question right the first time.

After he was assured that he is the right person, Abdul continued,

"We will go into details later if that's alright with you?"

"Now, I need details now!" Jonah asked, staring profoundly and sternly into his eyes. He might be an employee of a Prince, but Jonah was also not unimportant that he could be kept on a pedestal just like that. So he decided to probe further.

"So far, you have not explained your business, but I am intrigued. Abdul, or whatever your name is, you must tell me more prior to accepting this assignment, or this conversation is over. Is that agreeable with you?"

"That is good, very good," Abdul replied.

"First of all, who is your employer?" Jonah asked.

"I'm sorry, but I am not at liberty to say at this time, but he knows you," Abdul quickly responded as he continued, "I represent a man of, shall we say, of great wealth and power. He has certain interests that he is willing to sell that are something of great value. There are several others that are willing to participate in making an offer for this item, but since there are so many individuals, my employer suggested that we conduct a, shall we say *a private auction*."

Abdul continued, "Mr. Knight, due to the nature of this sale, my employer is willing to compensate you very generously. Also, are you willing to travel? All expenses will be paid for with an advance payment of one-half of the fee prior to your departure. The balance will be paid to you upon completion of the sale, as well as all expenses to return. All transportation will be provided."

"What or how much, Abdul?" Jonah asked, "How much and how will I be paid. I do not work for free, and my fee is quite high," Jonah said, thinking of no less than five hundred dollars.

Abdul replied, "I am allowed to offer you three thousand dollars if that is acceptable to you."

Jonah sat silently for a moment, trying to absorb what he was just told. The amount was far beyond what he had ever expected, and quite frankly, he was thrilled with the large amount offered.

Taking a moment to think things over, trying to hold his breath, he thought. That was more than he earned in four months of hard work around here. How come so much money for selling just one item? He thought to himself. Jonah thought this was a dream situation, and he should follow this to see where it will take him. Three thousand dollars, *WOW!* Fast money for a quick job, he thought. Stay calm and collected. Do not seem overly anxious, he thought.

"Travel, where?" he inquired. This might be an opportunity to see what some other places he saw pictures of in the books that Flagstaff showed him, instead of Kansas, Missouri, Chicago, and Oklahoma City. Jonah thought, maybe New York. It all seems a bit suspicious. Why me? Questions were running through his mind, so many questions must be answered.

Responding in a very calm voice, "The financial payment will be sufficient," Jonah said. "Where would this auction be held, and how long will I be gone?" Jonah asked.

"Approximately six to seven days," Abdul said, avoiding the destination. "You will be contacted shortly with the details and travel documents. Of course, a portion will be advanced on your fee. It will be paid at that time, so you can, if you choose, settle any of your financial matters. Is that

"That would be acceptable to me. When will I be leaving?" Jonah asked. The response was surprising to Jonah.

"You will be contacted by a man by the name of Hammond, Mr. Albert Hammond. Mr. Hammond is preparing the appropriate documents and funds for you. He will contact you in a few days. Please be prepared to leave at that time; after all, *time is of the essence.* I will contact my employer and let him know that you have agreed to our arrangement. Please be ready as time really is a factor of significance. We must be prompt and on schedule. Is that agreeable to you, Mr. Knight?"

Jonah agreed with the terms Abdul answered with a firm conviction and satisfaction that he had completed his mission. He shook Jonah's hand and said, "Agreed then."

Jonah asked, "Will I see you again?" Jonah asked.

"When you arrive at the destination, I will meet you. Please, Mr. Knight, please do not mention this arrangement or our meeting or my visit to anyone. Your integrity in matters like this must be at the highest level. No one, Mr. Knight, absolutely no one must know of this conversation and our arrangement. Can I count on you for maintaining the strictest confidentially?"

"I understand, and you can count on it," Jonah said.

"Thank you, Mr. Knight. I will see you again when you arrive at the destination." Abdul answered while sipping his tea. Jonah recalled what he was told and wanted to know more on the context, so he asked,

"By the way, you said that someone recommended me. Who was it?"

"That I cannot tell you, but you came highly recommended by a man that did a lot of work for my employer's father and his friends, also he was a particularly good friend to me. His name was, I'm sorry. Currently, I am not at liberty to say, but I can tell you this, you live in his house, don't you, Mr. Knight?" Abdul answered.

Jonah was startled, just stared at him for a moment. He was not sure but was learning a little bit more about his mentor, Peter Flagstaff. Something about the statement made him happy as for so long, he heard nothing new about the person who made him all that he was today.

Jonah recalled, how every time Flagstaff went away, sometimes for weeks at a time, and when Flagstaff would return home from one of those mysterious trips, he would go silent for a day or so.

Abdul finished his tea and stood up, thanked Jonah for his time, and vanished as quickly as he appeared, climbing into the waiting black Buick sedan parked near the front of the Café, driving rapidly down the street, out of sight.

As Jonah walked back to the house, his mind could not help but wonder about his mentor. He joined the path of his reminiscence back to where it was broken by Abdul's departure.

He continued to try and figure out why he was so meticulous in teaching him. Jonah noticed and now realized that Peter Flagstaff was a very mysterious and special man indeed.

When he returned from some of his journeys, Doc Swenson would come over, and they would go upstairs into his bedroom carrying his medical bag and immediately close the door.

Sometimes, he would notice many scars, like bullet holes or knife wounds, closed; sealed upon his chest, shoulders, and back when he would remove his shirt.

"Where did you get those?" he would ask when his shirt was off, only to be abruptly yelled at, "Mind your own fucken business boy, get out," immediately slamming the door loudly.

10.

CHAPTER TEN

Peter Flagstaff had a varied collection of pistols, both automatics, revolvers, and his trusty Winchester Double action shotgun always loaded in a convenient spot around the house and close to his desk.

He always thought that he was just a popular local auctioneer just grinding out a living, taking a lot of short vacations. *Who was this guy anyway*, he questioned himself? Peter Flagstaff was fearless. He stood up to everybody in town, and they respected and probably feared him for it.

Jonah certainly was learning more about the local neighborhood auctioneer, which reminded him of one other thing about Peter that was unknown to him.

He promised Peter that he would never enter the mysterious room in the basement, but now is the time. He died, leaving everything to me.

His curiosity finally got the best of him. Jonah spent hours searching the house in all the hidden corners, nooks, crannies, and cabinets, finally realizing Flagstaff would always hide things in plain sight.

The words that Flagstaff kept repeating as he was teaching him kept resonating through his head, "Always remember that some, if not most important things are hidden in plain sight."

He stopped spinning around in the office chair and just stared around the room, analyzing everything within his view. A plain sight, he thought, hidden in plain sight.

Frustrated, sitting in the living room staring at the fireplace, staring at the lamp. Peter always said he liked the lamp just where it was told never to move it.

He jumped up and went over to the fireplace, slowly running his hands across the carved ornate wooden mantle, placing the oil lamp on the table.

He felt something strange as he ran hands to either side across the top; something was wrong, running his hand forward and backwards from one end to the other.

A small three-inch hole, with a piece of matching, chipped wood covering it, directly in the center, precisely just below where the lamp was placed.

After removing the hand-knitted white filigreed linen cloth and the small piece of wood, the hole contained two hidden keys, neatly placed in the gouged-out pocket under the base in a small hole dug into the mantle. The unusual oil lamp located on the fireplace was a perfect hiding place. *What a genius*, he thought about Flagstaff.

His blood was running faster as he rapidly headed towards the stairs leading to the basement. His anticipation was building as the adrenaline was rushing in veins. He came to a realization that he never thought much about the concrete room until he met Abdul.

Flicking the light switch on, he proceeded down the stairs to the steel door. Brushing away the cobwebs, he fumbled with the rusty tight locks testing out which key perfectly fits which particular lock, pulling them open.

Since Jonah never went down into the basement, he never thought about it. Therefore, he was excited to finally find out what was in the room he was forbidden to enter.

The slightly rusty door hinges creaked as he pulled it open. Once opened, he looked around for another light switch.

Searching the walls, Jonah found a small light switch on the right side of the wall, which he turned on.

The room lit up as if four new street lamps were placed on every wall around the room. He took a deep breath, gasping at what he saw.

There were neatly wrapped plastic bags neatly stacked in the center of the room and several other small black bags tied with jute string. There were two large locked cabinets standing almost proudly up against the wall. Absolutely everything was wrapped tightly to keep any unwanted air or moisture away from destroying the contents.

Fitting the newfound keys in the lock on the cabinet, he opened the wooden oak doors. He found an array of rifles, pistols, and knives of all sorts. All are clean, loaded, and ready to kill anything that gets in their way. Each one polished almost to a mirror finish. All the rifles were loaded and ready for use too.

The other cabinet contained other packages, which he opened very carefully. There were stacks of twenty, fifty, and one-hundred-dollar bills neatly tied in bundles.

Sitting on the top of the waist-high cabinet located in the middle of the room was a large manila envelope with the note: "OPEN ONLY UPON MY DEATH."

Jonah slowly opened the envelope to find a letter addressed to him.

"If you are reading this, I have died or am no longer alive. You have found the hidden keys, opened the door in the basement and started to go through everything that I have accumulated for many years. You were the son that I never had.

Jonah, everything that I have is now yours. You have been a wonderful companion to me and helped me considerably in my life. Although I am not a teacher by trade, I thoroughly enjoyed teaching you what I know and more.

I recommended you to other people that might contact you for your services in another country. Be very careful and watch your back, always.

One man will protect you. I passed your name on to a very good friend of mine in the Middle East who will contact you for a service one day. This man you can trust but always be very cautious.

He is a Prince in Saudi Arabia. His father was a King and a very good friend of mine but, unfortunately, died before his time. His son, Najib, was also his student and was prepared to take over the running of the family businesses.

I am reminding you again to be very careful out there. My life has been very difficult, and I have made many enemies trying to kill me. There might be a chance that they will try to get you too as revenge.

There is enough money for you to disappear and to go somewhere else and start fresh. If you decide to remain, keep a gun handy. Remember, *trust no one.* Under the desk, there is a pistol. On the right side, under the bottom of the false drawer to protect you if you need it.

Remember everything that I taught you.

Do not spend all this money. Live modestly and hide your wealth.

I love you, my son, Peter."

Jonah read the letter several times and teared up on the last line. The letter made him realize how they loved each other in silence. He, too, loved Peter as the Father that he never had.

11.

CHAPTER ELEVEN

Five days passed since the conversation with Abdul. There hasn't been any contact by anyone. Just a hoax, he thought. Someone was trying to play a trick on him, which he did not appreciate at all. However, something in his gut told him to be patient. For sure, something will happen soon, he thought.

As the day wore on and entered into the night, he was sitting at his desk doing paperwork for Hays National; when a loud knock at the door startled him.

He noticed that the time was ten minutes to eleven. "It's open; come in," Jonah said. His gun was readily available placed on his lap for fear that someone might try to rob or kill him.

"Mr. Jonah Knight, I presume." The stranger said.

"My name is Albert Hammond. Breezy out there, isn't it? Mind if I come in?" Pushing his way into the house past Jonah, "Mind if I have a seat so we can get started." He said as he plumped down on the chair in front of the desk.

Hammond was approximately five foot nine' tall, middle-aged. Probably around fifty, Jonah guessed. He was wearing a dark grey double-breasted suit, and a white shirt opened at the collar with his tie hanging off to the side. His hair was salt and pepper coloring, slightly mussed due to the winds, which started to pick up outside. His footwear was black western boots with silver covers on the toes of the boots.

He continued, "I have been instructed to contact you with some documents. Are you Jonah Knight?"

"Yes, yes I am," he replied.

"Hey, got some water? I'm parched." Hammond pulled up the wooden chair from the corner of the room up to his desk.

"Sign here by the X prior to our continuing this conversation, OK? It's on page two. Just simple stuff, you know, the usual shit they put down on paper."

Hammond pushed the papers across the desk for Jonah's review and signature. "It's ok. Your initials will do."

"It's my boss's instructions. Sorry about that, privacy stuff, you know. After we talk a bit, you gotta sign a contract, nothing special, just so you know that you do your thing and we pay you for, got it?"

Hammond pushed the papers in front of him, lighting a cigarette, taking a deep drag, blowing smoke rings in the air as he exhaled. "Oops, sorry, mind if I smoke?"

"Okay, sure," Jonah replied, thinking of how useless are his questions being directed towards him after the action was already done as if his opinion was being taken under consideration here. He was annoyed with doing this before receiving anything.

"It's just a receipt for the advance payment and the confidential agreement and what we're going to talk about, okay? Thanks."

"We have to get the paperwork out of the way first, okay?" Hammond seems like a guy who spoke fast and got the work done even faster, *a doer and not a talker*.

After signing the paperwork, making sure that he signed on the line at the bottom of both pages, Hammond continued, "Okay there, pal, here are your instructions, travel documents, and the advance payment of fifteen hundred bucks in cash on your fee as agreed. It's all there, buddy boy, no need to count it. The balance will be paid to you upon completion of the sale. If you do a good job, you might get a bonus. You ready to leave now?" Hammond asked.

"Want some help? Remember, time is of the essence; we must be at the airport within the hour. My car is just outside to take us there. Anything else that you need will be provided. Are you ready now, Mr. Knight? We must leave on time," Hammond insisted. "Time is really important."

Jonah grabbed a small duffle bag he prepared placed near the door in case this was really going to happen. He locked the house, leaving a note for the new housekeeper, Sarah Ferguson.

Jonah climbed into the back seat of the waiting black Cadillac Fleetwood sedan. As soon as the door closed, the driver quickly sped off into the night.

The windows in the car were covered with shades so no one could see in or out. Jonah remembered what Abdul had said; *this was a very secretive mission*. No one, he thought, no one can see me leaving. Only the housekeeper knew that he would be gone for approximately seven or eight days or something like that. He was specific in his instructions to her. This recalled him of how things were when Flagstaff used to leave. It felt like history was repeating itself!

They raced down the back road as not to be seen. Neither the driver nor Hammond spoke during the trip. The car headed straight for the small remote airport where a private plane was waiting, engines running.

"Are you coming with me?" Jonah asked.

Hammond said, "Nope, not this trip. Someone will be waiting for you at the destination. I implore you, Mr. Knight; please do not speak with or to anyone regarding your journey. You will be watched closely. Now, you must leave. Have a good flight." Hammond handed the bag to the woman flight attendant on the plane, and without another word, he turned, jumped into the waiting car, and sped off into the empty space of the night.

Jonah never flew before and was quite nervous and excited at the same time. As soon as he climbed the steps, the door slammed shut behind him, jolting the plane slightly.

"Please sit down and fasten your buckle, Sir," said the woman flight attendant. "My name is Alexis; I will be taking care of you during your flight. If there is anything you need, please do not hesitate to ask me, Mr. Knight, okay? Please use the buckle on the seat, will you?"

"Yes, of course, Thank you," he replied.

She walked to the back of the plane, sat down, put on her seat belt, grabbed a book, and relaxed.

The engines started to roar as the plane began to move. Rolling down to the end of the runway, slowing down, the engines became louder, shaking the plane. It started to move faster, picking up speed as it rolled down the runway, finally lifting off, soaring upward into black night skies.

When the plane seemed to level off, he looked around to see who else was aboard. The other seats were empty except for one other man sitting near the back; he was the only other passenger on the plane. He didn't say anything, just acknowledged his presence. He kept to himself for the entire flight.

Once in the air, "Alexis," he called, "do you have anything to drink?"

"What would you prefer, Sir?" she answered.

"What about a good glass of wine," he asked.

"Thank you," he replied as she walked down the aisle to satisfy his need.

Alexis was an exotic-looking woman, approximately 24 years old, Jonah guessed. Her voice was soft but firm in a kind, sweet way. She stood five foot, four inches tall with slightly high cheekbones only accentuated by her dark, mysterious-looking eyes. Her hair was long, almost black in color, appearing silky in texture. Jonah could not stop looking at her features.

He has never seen a woman so beautiful. Her figure was like an hourglass, so perfect and well proportioned. She was wearing a dark gray skirt, a white blouse buttoned up to her neck, and a tightly buttoned jacket that was fitted just below her buttocks. Her legs were slim and looked like she just slid into her black shoes with a large two-inch narrow heel as she walked gracefully down the aisle. She was beautiful, a perfect display of a woman that he had ever seen.

Jonah had a hard time trying not to stare and to be polite, but he wanted to keep talking to her, so he kept the conversations rather on the light side.

Alexis told him to relax as this was going to be a long flight.

As he relaxed, he reached into his inside jacket pocket, took the sealed letter from Peter, opened it, and started to read it again.

Alexis walked up to Jonah and announced, "In approximately three hours, we will be landing in upstate

New York for refueling, then on to your destination. Mr. Knight, you will be allowed off the plane for safety's sake until it is ready to leave. Someone will meet you at the bottom of the stairs and stay with you. He will have a warm meal and something to drink. Thank you for your cooperation; please stay in your seat until we land, please," she said.

Alexis sat down in the rear of the plane with a magazine and didn't say another word until the plane landed.

Approximately three hours later, the plane started its descent. Lower and lower it went, circling around in the air, finally landing at a small airport.

The plane finally came to a stop in front of a large corrugated steel building. The door opened when a tall, lanky man in blue overalls boarded. "Mr. Knight, please follow me," he said. They both went down the stairs and into the building and moved toward an office. There, on the desk, was a feast fit for a king, with salad, broiled chicken, potatoes, vegetables, and a piece of apple pie for dessert. "Would you like water or wine, or something else, sir?" said the man in overalls.

"Water would be fine, thank you," Jonah replied. He didn't want to be lightheaded, or yet, he was afraid of being drugged.

Looking at the plane, he noticed that the other passenger on the plane walked down the stairs to a waiting car, and another man climbed aboard.

Finally, after an hour, Jonah boarded the plane, and they were off. Looking out the window, he noticed that when they were in the air, all the lights at the airport vanished as if someone turned off the light switch as they disappeared into the black starlit night skies.

Alexis handed him a pillow and blanket, suggesting Jonah take a nap since it will be several hours before they arrive at the destination.

Everybody always mentioned the word "destination." His curiosity was certainly peaked as nobody said anything beyond that.

"Where are we going?" he asked. Not giving him the satisfaction of an answer, she just smiled and walked to the rear of the plane, sat down on one of the seats, pulled a blanket over her fluffing a pillow, and proceeded to doze off in a deep sleep. Jonah did the same.

12.

CHAPTER TWELVE

"Wake up, Mr. Knight," shaking him lightly. "We are preparing to land. Fasten your seat belt, please."

"Thank you, Alexis."

The plane circled the airport for a few minutes descending lower, finally touching the ground smoothly as if it was gliding on ice.

Upon arrival, two black Mercedes Benz limousines followed the plane. When the aircraft stopped, each one parking on either side of the plane, guiding it to the farthest hanger on the field. A large building painted black with a large gold leaf emblem painted on the front doors of the hanger.

The doors opened like a whale waiting to swallow its prey. As the plane slowly roared into the building, the doors closed behind us as the engines stopped humming, and then, silence. Complete privacy. *What's going on?* He questioned himself.

When she opened the door, a familiar face appeared on the stairway. Abdul started to say, "Mr. Knight, I am so happy that you finally arrived. Everyone is looking forward to meeting you. We must go now to the palace. Please follow me," as he grabbed the duffle bag from Alexis.

As Jonah was starting to leave the plane, he looked at the other passenger getting up from his seat. Abdul nodded to the man as he descended from the plane. Jonah looked at Alexis like a lost puppy and spoke, "Alexis," he said and was immediately interrupted, "do not worry, Mr. Knight, everything is going to be okay."

"Will I see you again?" He asked. "Most assuredly, you can count on it," was her response as she turned back into the interior of the plane.

A man was holding the rear door open for us to enter the limousine. It had a dark, rich tan leather interior, with, of all things, a fully stocked liquid bar filled with a large bottle of water and two soft drink bottles in the bar located on the back of the front seat.

There was another man wearing a black suit on the front passenger side. A bodyguard, he thought. As we climbed into the back seat, the curtains were pulled shut. A second Mercedes stayed close to the rear of the Limo. It followed closely behind, not allowing anything to get between the cars.

"Abdul, who was that other man on the plane?" he quizzed.

"He was there to make sure that there were no problems and you were safe. Is that okay with you?" was his response.

Jonah sat silently as the car sped through the streets.

Abdul started the conversation in a very soft and pleasant tone.

"Mr. Knight, please excuse the privacy issues, but we are protecting you the best that we can," Abdul continued. We will be arriving at the palace shortly, where hopefully, you will find the accommodations to your satisfaction."

"When will I meet your employer?" Jonah asked. "Tomorrow morning, you will be having breakfast together," Abdul said.

As they sped through the streets, the limousine pulled up to two fifteen-foot-tall ornate gates in what appeared to be painted with gold and black paint.

They were pushed open by two men dressed in white Phatui Kurta standing outside the gates waiting for the cars to arrive. Each one had an automatic rifle across their back. As quickly as they entered the courtyard, the gates closed quickly.

When Jonah got out of the car, he was speechless as he looked around the courtyard. His eyes widened as he had never imagined such a magnificent structure. He counted four stories high. Each opening around the plaza had arches with pillars of which the likes he had never seen, not even in magazines.

Jonah was immediately greeted by two men dressed in long white coats and matching pants that appeared to be made of a silk-like material with rimless white caps.

"Welcome, Mr. Knight, welcome," one said in broken English. "Please follow me. I'll take your bag, sir," said the other, each man trying to please him.

They walked through the extensive garden to a winding stairway, up to two flights of stairs. They proceeded down a long hallway stopping at a large double door. The other servant opened both doors.

"Mr. Knight, my name is Habib, and my companion is Omar. Please, Mr. Knight, enter. This will be your room during your stay with us. Please do not hesitate to ask for anything to make your stay as comfortable as possible."

As the doors opened, Jonah stood there, amazed at the large room. It was the most elegant thing that Jonah has ever seen or imagined. A large bed with fine linen fit for a king ornately carved gold chairs in every corner. The bathroom displayed gold faucets on the sink, toilet, and bathtub. The tile floors were pictures in mosaic artwork that were designed throughout. The finest of picturesque tapestries were hung on each of the walls.

Abdul followed Jonah into the room as Omar watched from the doorway. Jonah could have never imagined anything like this, he thought, keeping his emotions in, trying not to display too much excitement.

"Can I get you anything?" Abdul asked.

"No, no, thank you," Jonah replied. "When you freshen up, I will give you a tour of the gardens and part of the palace. Would you like to do that, Mr. Knight?"

"Yes, yes, thank you," was Jonah's eager reply.

"Would you like to change into something more comfortable? I'm sure that since you are not accustomed to the rather warm weather. We have something more comfortable for you in the wardrobe," Omar asked.

"Thank you. It will be just a moment. I'll change," Jonah replied.

When he opened the doors to the closet, there were clothes that he certainly was not accustomed to wearing. White shirts and pants, slippers, and a few belts.

The tour of the gardens lasted approximately one hour, as he walked slowly, looking at all the unbelievable flowers and mosaic tile work. They proceeded into the house, where he saw the great room, hallways, and the library. The volume of artwork spattered on the walls. Massive gold filigree frames surrounded each one. There were almost as many tapestries made with silver and gold threads as he had ever seen. Never in his wild dreams could Jonah ever imagine anything like this.

Abdul approached Jonah, "Mr. Knight, you must be tired after your long trip. Omar and Habib will be your personal assistants for the duration of your stay at the palace. They will walk you back to your room and will wake you at eight in the morning. Breakfast will be served on the patio just off the great room at nine promptly.

The clothes you are to wear to breakfast are on the bed. Good night, Mr. Knight, see you in the morning." Abdul left promptly as both servants assigned to him walked him to his room.

13.

CHAPTER THIRTEEN

A loud knock at the door came exactly at Eight AM as Abdul had said…

"Mr. Knight, "It is time for breakfast. Shall we prepare your bath, or would you prefer a shower, sir?"

"Shower is fine, thank you." This is what the better things in life are, he thought, remembering Flagstaff. He would be proud of him. Having someone to cater to your every need, for everything, he thought. Wait a minute, he thought, I think that Peter was here a few times for sure.

Omar handed him two large, very soft terry cloth white towels. After his shower in the golden mosaic tiled shower stall, Jonah looked for his clothes, which must have disappeared during the night.

"Where are my clothes?" Jonah asked Omar.

Habib responded, "We removed them for sizing and cleaning after your long flight. Other clothing has been provided for the breakfast meal. Please hurry, Mr. Knight, the Prince will be waiting," one said.

Jonah dressed in a white shirt with white pants and slippers that were provided.

Silently Jonah followed the two servants down the stairs to the patio where Abdul and his employer were already seated sipping tea.

Abdul rose on his feet, "Mr. Knight, welcome. Please sit down here at the end of the table. Please, may I introduce Prince Najib," Abdul said.

"Ahh, Mr. Knight, it is such a pleasure to finally meet you," as they both got up to shake hands. "Please, please, sit down."

"Excuse me, Prince, were you the guy from the hotel in Chicago?"

"Ah, you remembered me as I remembered you. I am forever in your debt."

"Please just call me, Najib. My servants call me Prince. What may I call you, Mr. Knight?"

"Jonah is fine," he replied.

He was twenty-seven years old, around Jonah's age, six-foot-tall, fair skin color, and a full head of thick black hair. He was very handsome, clean-shaven, and dressed in a light blue colored sports jacket with white pants. He had three rings on his right hand and one on the left.

"What would you like to eat, Jonah?"

"Anything is fine, thank you," Jonah replied. As the Prince clapped his hands, the servants proceeded to serve various food items, the kind of which Jonah has never seen or even tasted before. The conversations were general and light in nature.

After breakfast, Najib said, "Go away and now leave us alone," as the servants hurriedly picked up the gold-plated dishes and crystal glassware, placed them on a cart, and scrambled to leave the room promptly.

"First of all, do you have any questions for me?" Najib asked.

"Where am I?" Jonah asked. "Everything has been kept very secret. Let's start there, OK?" Jonah asked.

Najib responded, "You are just on the outside of Cairo, Egypt, at one of my residences. You traveled here on my private plane. What we are about to discuss is of an important nature. I am sorry for the privacy and secrecy, but you will be selling something very expensive. There are a lot of people that will be unhappy that they were outbid and may become, shall we say, not pleased in the least."

"What happens if an argument starts or trouble erupts?" Jonah questioned.

Najib replied, "Some of the bidders will think that it is you that caused the failure, selling to someone else instead of them. If there is a disruption, my armed guards who will be posted around the room will make sure that you are safe and that everything goes smoothly."

"I would like to know what I will be selling; how many buyers will be there, and where will the sale take place?" Jonah asked promptly.

"The sale will take place tomorrow at noon on the other side of the city in a room that I specifically designed for this purpose. You will be selling four identical Diamonds, each one four carats in size. Have you sold diamonds before? They are flawless and considered priceless. I expect the sale will bring approximately one million each, or four million for the set. Have you ever sold diamonds before, Jonah?"

"Not like these," he replied. "Can I see them?"

"Absolutely," as Najib called one of the servants to fetch them. "My servants are very loyal to me at all times. I pay them well and take care of their families. I do believe that they would take a bullet for me."

Three men, one carrying the stones and the other two standing guards, approached them, presenting a medium-sized, brushed burled walnut box. Najib opened the black-lined velvet box to expose the most magnificent diamonds that Jonah had ever seen. They were almost blinding in the morning light. Jonah was completely speechless for a minute.

"Absolutely beautiful, just beautiful," Jonah said.

"Some of the Buyers know who you are or about you and are aware that you have arrived. They might try to stop you from making the sale, so I must insist that you remain in the palace until we are prepared to leave for the auction sale. Is it alright with you?" Najib asked.

"Yes, yes, of course," Jonah replied.

Abdul approached the Prince and whispered something in his ear.

"Now, I must beg your leave. I must attend to some unfinished business. I will see you for dinner. Jonah, my friend, this could be the beginning of a hopefully, very long relationship."

After another tour of the palace, Jonah returned to his room to get a nap before dinner. He still was tired from the trip and lag time from crossing the dateline. He brought a book to read before retiring to the bedroom.

Each of the windows were large and approximately 8 feet tall and six feet wide, with ornate carved wooden shutters.

Jonah opened the shutters on one window and could not even imagine the sights that he beheld as he looked out the window. It was fantastic; he could not stop staring at the gardens and the other parts of the house.

His clothes were returned later in the afternoon, washed, pressed, and hung on silk-wrapped wooden hangers, and the shoes were polished almost to a mirror finish, more than they were when he purchased them. This treatment was for sure something he never got before.

14.

CHAPTER FOURTEEN

Dinner was served promptly at five-thirty in the afternoon. The food that was displayed on the long, linen-covered dining table contained various salad items, lamb shank, couscous with wild mushrooms, herbs, and vegetables. There were two bottles of wine on the table, as well as a large pot of herbal tea.

Najib entered the dining hall a few minutes later with servants in tow.

"A great pleasure to see you again! Hopefully, you enjoyed your nap. Jonah, even though I practice a religion that forbids the consumption of alcoholic beverages, I do indulge, on special occasions, such as your arrival to my humble home and this special time."

After dinner was served, the servants cleared the table and left the room. Both men started to talk without formalities and about themselves. Jonah spoke about Hays, Kansas, and his life growing up, his parents, their deaths, the farm, and why he decided to become an Auctioneer. He talked about Peter Flagstaff and what kind of a father figure he was to him.

Najib commented that he has known Peter growing up and how he admired him, too. "He was a good friend of my Father."

Najib, without making any facial expressions, talked about his life and his parents. They loved him and were very caring. They made sure that he received the best education that is why he got a degree in business and finance from Oxford University at the insistence of both.

They talked about so many things well into the early evening. They bonded like brothers who got lost years back. Jonah never had a close friend, nor was he ever able to communicate to anyone his feelings or laughter.

Yes, Najib was going to be his first real friend, he thought. He never felt so comfortable with anyone. Both talked and laughed until five minutes past midnight. Nothing was out of bounds as they became very comfortable with each other.

"Jonah, we must retire from this most enjoyable evening. Tomorrow is going to be an inspiring day for both of us. Good night and I will see you in the morning. Habib will escort you to your room." They both gave each other a soft hug as if they finally found a long, lost friend.

15.

CHAPTER FIFTEEN

Jonah was awakened at eight-thirty the following morning as Omar entered the room. He opened the shutters to allow the light to yield to the morning sun.

"Good morning, Mr. Knight! It is time to prepare for the day. Your new suit is hanging on the armoire. Please try it on after your shower to make sure that it is sized properly."

The black tuxedo fitted him perfectly. He was given a white shirt with black studs with bright diamond centers. A black bow tie made of pure silk. The shoes were wingtip style, polished to a mirror finish.

Jonah was told that the Prince will meet him at the sale site due to some unfinished business, and they will be leaving at ten-thirty precisely. "Please be ready, Mr. Knight," Omar continued, "There is a small breakfast on the table for you to enjoy before we drive to the building."

Two cars entered the courtyard at ten-fifteen, where two men got out of each vehicle. They were wearing black suits in the hot, humid weather. One shouted out, "We are ready, Mr. Knight, please hurry. The Prince is waiting!"

16.

CHAPTER SIXTEEN

Two limousines sped through the streets, weaving in and out the barely paved roadway. Of course, having Prince Najib's flags and emblems on each of the limos helped a lot.

It took approximately twenty minutes to arrive at the auction site where the diamonds were to be sold. They drove into a specially built garage with concrete walls located under the building into a large private parking spot. The guardsmen got out of the cars with automatic weapons, each facing all the entrances.

Abdul opened the door, "Please, Mr. Knight, this way."

Jonah was rushed up the few stairs into what appeared to be a small anteroom adjacent to the hall's main room. Najib came in and hugged Jonah and kissed him on both cheeks.

"Are you ready?" he asked.

"Ready as ever," Jonah responded.

"We'll wait here until everybody is seated. First, they must have refreshments," Najib continued.

"At that time, I will be seated in my private box on your left. The auction will be all yours. I have the utmost confidence that you will bring the highest dollars for me. Good Luck, Jonah!" Najib said as he hurried out of the room.

Jonah and Abdul inspected the crowd through a twelve by twelve-inch, approximately 2" thick, bulletproof, and one-way window.

Abdul pointed out the people who would be very serious bidders and those he should keep an open eye on.

"They might be troublesome, be careful," Abdul warned. Everyone was seated and were becoming restless, speaking to one another in low whispers.

"I will introduce you and the diamonds, and then you will proceed. I'll be seated just behind you. Watch the numbers as they are raised, especially numbers 139 and 205," Abdul said.

They both walked down the narrow stairway to the rear of the stage section where the auction sale was to take place.

Abdul walked out to the microphone and started to address the crowd.

"Ladies and gentlemen, thank you all for coming to this once-in-a-lifetime event. You have all inspected the Diamonds with your gemologists and other professionals. You also have confirmed that they are not only real but also flawless. These are rare indeed; no duplicates are to be found anywhere in the world. Prince

Najib has graciously offered to sell them from his own private collection.

At this time, may I introduce Mr. Jonah Knight, who will be selling them to the highest bidder? They will be sold as a set and not individually. The winner will pay for their purchase immediately after the sale."

Jonah has never seen the myriad collection of people seated in the front of the podium in the plush red velvet chairs. He has always heard of the rich, but nothing like these nine women and sixteen men.

A few of the women wore veils over their heads and faces with long flowing gowns of what appeared to be of the finest of fabrics. They were wearing necklaces of diamonds, rubies, and sapphires. The other women wore long dresses with both large and small hats with long flowing black hair and high-heeled shoes. Their fingers and necks were covered with diamonds and emeralds.

Some of the men wore light-colored business suits with white turbans, while others wore long flowing robes with colored cloth covering their heads. Some had well-groomed beards, while some others had moustaches. A few were clean-shaven. Their suits appeared to be made of the finest materials available.

Jonah started, "Ladies and gentlemen, I am sure you have all inspected the diamonds to be sold. To remind you again, all of you have also confirmed that they are not only of the highest quality but indeed are flawless. As instructed and due to their rarity, they will not be sold individually, instead, you must purchase all four at the same price. Hopefully, that is understood by everyone. May we have an opening bid of two hundred thousand dollars for each stone?"

Najib was startled; "The price was far too low. Is he trying to give them away? I thought that he could be trusted?"

Abdul grabbed his shoulder, "Wait, my Prince, be patient. I have seen this man work, and he is very good. Trust your instincts, please, my Prince, please."

"Relax, my prince," Abdul told him, "I trust him to do the right thing. Let's see where this will go. He has a good reputation for the best dollars. I trust him, your highness." Wait and see, the Prince thought to himself. Let's see how this is going to play out.

"Thank you," said Jonah, as the first bidder raised his paddle.

"Now, five hundred thousand is bid," as he proceeded at a more rapid pace.

"Thank you, now who will bid seven-hundred for each of these scarce stones." Jonah noticed that Bidder 205 started to become slightly agitated and restless, shifting nervously in his seat. Abdul told him about this person and to watch out.

As the bidding started to accelerate faster, "I need nine hundred thousand," bidder 312 raised his paddle. Bidder number 122 walked out of the room with his entourage of four, in anger that the price was more than he was willing to spend.

Jonah continued, "Who will bid one million for each of these beautiful Diamonds? Quite rare indeed. You will never be able to duplicate these anywhere, *flawless*. This is an investment, I assure you. They will only increase in value in a rather short time." After a pause of silence, Bidder 229 raised the paddle, "thank you," Jonah said. "Now, we will separate the men from the boys."

"The bidding is now at one million looking for one million, one hundred thousand for these rare collectible Diamonds. Thank you," to Bidder 312, with a smile on his face as he was expecting no one to outbid him.

After a moment of silence, from the middle of the room, bidder 210, that has remained silent throughout the whole process, finally raised his paddle and yelled out,

"One million, three hundred," he said with a firm conviction in his voice.

He had a stern look on his face which looked like he was angry that he had to bid higher than anyone else to get the stones. The room was silent as they stared at him.

Bidder 205 was turning red with anger, appearing as if he was waiting for or to pick a fight.

"One million, three hundred fifty thousand, that is my final bid." Bidder 210 appeared to have a vendetta against 205 and was determined not to let him have them, raised his paddle, "one million, and five hundred thousand," smiling as if he won the game.

"We need one million six hundred thousand to raise and to continue with the bidding," Jonah said with a firm controlling voice.

"If all bids are in, anyone else, going once," he said, pausing for a moment, "Going twice," with a slight pause, "Any further bidding? If not, these rare precious stones will be sold to bidder 210 for one million, five hundred thousand. From the rear of the room, a bidder paddle number 214 was raised, "Two Million!"

"The total is now eight million for the complete set. Thank you," Jonah said loudly.

"Are there any further bid for these very rare diamonds that will certainly increase in value over a short period of time?" Jonah stated with a firm-sounding voice. A little louder to make sure that everyone else in the room pays more attention.

"I hear no one, I will pronounce this sale closed, and the Diamonds are sold to the gentleman in the last row, Bidder 214."

Again, Jonah raised his voice, "SOLD!"

17.

CHAPTER SEVENTEEN

Thank you all for coming as Jonah stepped back and Abdul approached the podium. Mr. Sabah, please pay for your purchase as soon as possible, and thank you."

"Gladly," he said as he walked to the man in the front of the room.

"Tell Prince Najib that I will send my assistant for the stones with the payment later on this afternoon." Bowing towards the booth where Najib is sitting, as he walked out, talking with the six other people in his entourage.

"Wait a minute," shouted bidder 205. "Those diamonds are mine. You cheated me, you bastard. They are mine, and I want them now. You want more money; you know I've got it, ok, I'll give you the two million. I have the money, and I want the stones, *NOW!*" he shouted.

Jonah turned and said firmly, "Sir, I'm sorry, but the sale has been concluded. It is over. When I called for the bid, you sat there without countering the last bid. It is now over, and the diamonds are sold. There was time, and you missed the opportunity; the sale is over!"

Two of his bodyguards started to open their coats, showing their guns, "You cheated me you, God Damn Son of a Bitch, I'm going to get you for this, Knight! Fuck you Najib, you are a thief and a crook," he shouted.

Jonah was getting very nervous since guns were drawn. Najib's guards pointed their guns at the bodyguards.

Abdul quickly rushed in and grabbed Jonah, pulling him out and into the bulletproof anteroom for his protection. Two shots rang out; then there was silence.

Najib's bodyguards also fired shots. One-shot in the air as a warning and the other, a direct hit into Bidder 205's first bodyguard. Two guardsmen, one mortally wounded, and the other one slowly dropped his gun, picked his partner up, dragged his body, and walked backward out of the building. Everybody else that remained in the room dropped to the floor in fear of being shot. No one else wants to be shot or let alone get killed because of some madman.

"I WON'T FORGET YOU, KNIGHT. I'LL GET MY REVENGE, JUST WAIT AND SEE, YOU FUCKER, YOUR TIME WILL COME," he shouted as he hurriedly ran out of the room.

They were the parting words he shouted as he ran out of the building under cover and into his waiting

Mercedes limousine. The wounded bodyguard walked backward, dragging the other.

He left one man lying on the street, bleeding to death as they sped off into the crowded streets of the city.

"Who was that guy?" Jonah asked Abdul.

"His name is Ramon Sanchez from Madrid. He made his money from doing everything illegal, including a small side business of prostitution, gambling, drugs, mercenary killing, and even slave trading. He's quite ruthless and a man to be feared by most, but not the Prince," Abdul said. "We can handle him. We've done it in the past."

The Prince vanished as soon as the excitement started. His personal guards rushed him out immediately to return to safety in the Palace.

"Please, Mr. Knight, we must go now. Please follow me quickly," Abdul said in a firm voice. They raced quickly down the staircase to the waiting limousine, climbed in, and went speeding off to the

Palace, returning at 2:35 P.M.

18.

CHAPTER EIGHTEEN

Jonah has conducted many auctions over the years, but never where anybody was killed. Hope that on the next one, it won't be so bad. Sure, it was exciting, though, he thought to himself.

"Would you like to get some rest and get into something more comfortable to wear?" Abdul asked.

"Yes, thank you. When will I see the Prince?" Jonah asked.

"At the dinner hour, Mr. Knight, around six; will that be alright with you?" Abdul responded. "Yes, yes, of course, that will be fine," Jonah replied.

Jonah went up to his room for a nap and quickly fell asleep. Totally exhausted from all the excitement and the remaining jet lag.

One of the servants knocked on the door at five fifteen. "Mr. Knight, it is time for you to get up. Would you like to shower before dinner?"

Yes, thank you. I'll be ready in a half-hour." Jonah responded.

Jonah found his way to the main dining room, where the Prince was already eating some hummus and flatbread.

"JONAH," Najib shouted like a person he hasn't seen in years with a large smile. "Jonah, my friend, you are here," as he ran up to him very excitedly.

"Now that was thrilling, wasn't it?" Najib said with a hardy laugh.

"You were everything that I thought you were. You sold the Diamonds for eight million; that's over four million more than I expected. You have made me a very,

very happy man. You will stay over for a few days as my guest, please, I insist. Anything you would like will be my pleasure to supply you. Do not hesitate to ask for anything, OK?" Najib said.

During dinner, they talked about the auction and how it worked, and what happened.

"There was nothing special about the diamonds, just that they were a perfectly matched set," Najib said, "I started rumors about the stones about six months ago to enhance the value. Just a ploy to bring up the price," Najib said laughingly.

"I got them from a person that owed me a lot of money, so he paid up the debt in diamonds. A good deal, wouldn't you say?"

It was nine o'clock in the evening, tired from the day's activities, and the Prince decided to retire early. After bidding Jonah, a good night, Najib disappeared down the hallway.

Jonah was too wound up and couldn't even think of going to sleep right away. He went to his room, undressed, crawled on the bed, and prepared to read a book that he brought with him, "To Kill a Mockingbird," when there was a soft knock at the door.

"Who is it," he replied.

As he opened the door, she said, "My name is Nadia. I am a gift from the Prince. May I come in?" He opened the door to find a young, beautiful woman standing there pushing her way into the room. "Good evening, Mr. Knight!"

She was twentyish, he guessed, wearing nothing but a thin long, white silk gown, wrapped softly, flowing thinly, and covering her five-feet-tall frame. It was easy to see her beautiful figure through the glossy sheer fabric.

"Please, Mr. Knight, may I spend the night?" Nadia asked. How could Jonah resist? Her body was magnificently sculptured like a statue, the perfect poise of a female figure.

Closing the door and without saying a word, she touched his chest softly, pulling him closer, kissing him gently on his lips. Their mouths widened as their tongues touched, caressing each other. She placed his hands on her breasts, holding them firmly closed around each, as she made soft moaning sounds of pleasure. She took his hand, slowly turning and pulling him over to the waiting bed.

She was completely in charge of everything. All he could do is to be directed anyway she wanted. This woman was in complete control of the evening.

Laying on the bed's edge, Nadia placed his hand on her inner thigh, where she moved his hand slightly in an up and down motion pushing one finger inside of her. Pushing herself away, she slowly rose to her feet and did a sultry dance for him, touching and caressing his hair and face.

As Jonah watched, Nadia slowly removed the gown that covered her finely sculptured body. Her breasts stood up straight like they were positioned to shoot like cannons. They are so beautiful, he thought. The women at home never looked like this.

She knelt on the bed, slowly removing his bedclothes, caressing his body with every movement. As his manhood was growing, she slowly rubbed his erect unit for a moment and released him. Nadia held him closer to her body as she lay across his being, gently running her hands through his hair. Turning over on her back, she put his erect manhood inside with soft moaning sounds of pleasure.

"Do not worry, Mr. Knight; I will be here all night. I am here to please you," she said softly.

As Jonah moved his hips up and down faster, she pushed him back, saying, "Slower, please, I want to enjoy this as much as you."

This woman was well versed in the art of making love to a man. Nadia knew where and when to rub his nipples tight and softly. She was soft and gentle and knew where and how to touch a man. They made love several times during the night.

Jonah woke late, tired from the late-night activities. Nadia must have left sometime during the early morning. She was never to be seen again, at least not by him. Jonah will not forget this woman very easily.

19.

CHAPTER NINETEEN

The early warm morning sun shone brightly through the large, filigreed carved wooden shutters adorning each window. The silent heat only swirled by the two white fans on the ceiling.

The following day after breakfast, Najib decided that Jonah should see the city in his bulletproof limo with two of the rather large armed guards in the front seat for protection. Jonah was wondering when he would be paid the remainder of the fee that was promised. After all, he didn't want to offend his newfound friend.

After dinner on the second day after the eventful day, Najib started the conversation. "Jonah," he said, "I cannot thank you enough for what you have done for me. At first, I was not sure what you were going to do, but you surprised me. I must leave on emergency business this afternoon, but before I go, I would like to show you my appreciation by presenting you the final sum due, as agreed."

Najib called Abdul to bring the final payment. Abdul brought in a cigar-sized carved, burled walnut box.

As he handed the box to Jonah, "Open it," Najib said with a smile on his face.

When Jonah opened the box, he was expecting the balance of the twenty-five hundred due him.

For the first time, Jonah was completely speechless. Inside the box were fifteen thousand dollars and a gold embossed carved ring. This special ring had the Prince's emblem engraved on it and an impressive diamond stone to commemorate their meeting and for doing a spectacular job.

"I hope that you are satisfied with your fee," Najib said.

He just stared into the box for a moment, "Yes, yes, thank you. You are most generous. Thank you again."

"I have many friends elsewhere also that will protect anyone wearing this ring when you have a problem, any problem or situation in my country, show them this ring, and you will be protected," Najib said.

"Tomorrow morning Abdul will take you to my airport for your travel home. Now I have some important business to take care of so I must beg your leave. Jonah, with your permission, I would like to refer you to a few of my friends that possibly may have a similar situation. They would like to sell items of a, umm, different nature. They would also be very generous in payment for your services. May I do that for you, my friend? Can I call you *my dear friend?*"

"Yes, you can, my friend. Thank you very much, it would be appreciated. Najib, thank you for your friendship and the, umm, special gift," Jonah replied.

Abdul approached Najib and whispered in his ear. His face changed from pleasure to very serious. Najib stood up; gave Jonah a hug, kissed him on both cheeks, as was custom, and left promptly. As he was walking out, Najib shouted, "See you soon," as he rapidly disappeared down the long hallway.

After he left, Abdul said, "The Prince has many friends around the world. I'm sure that someone will contact you soon. Mr. Knight, the Prince always takes care of his people, of which you are now included. You are a very lucky man, a very lucky man indeed."

20.

CHAPTER TWENTY

The following morning at Eight A.M. sharp, Omar came with the familiar knock at the door. "Mr. Knight, It is time to go. Will you be ready soon?"

"Give me 15 minutes," Jonah said. The servants entered the room and proceeded to pack his bag for the trip home.

Promptly at Eight-thirty, they were on the way to the limo headed for the airport. Thirty minutes later, the limo pulled into the hanger where the plane was waiting to take him on his journey home.

"Thank you, Mr. Knight, for your services to the Prince. He will not forget what you have done for him.

He is a very generous man and a very good person to have on your side. He protects all of his friends," Abdul said.

Omar threw the small bag containing Jonah's belongings on the plane and drove off, leaving Jonah to board. When he placed his right foot on the stairs, Alexis appeared to be at the top of the stairs.

"Welcome aboard, Mr. Knight. I have been looking forward to seeing you again," Alexis said with a large smile on her face.

As Jonah looked up, he smiled as if he was a child with a new toy, saying, "Me too," as he proceeded up the stairs. There were two men casually dressed sitting in the last seats on the plane.

For the first time, Jonah saw the two pilots as they boarded. They were dressed in white shirts with epaulets with black stripes on each shoulder. Black pants and ties, polished shoes, and a cap displaying the Princes' emblems. They were talking to each other in

Arabic as they headed straight for the cockpit without saying a word to either Alexis or Jonah.

Alexis sat in the seat next to Jonah, reminding him to buckle up as the plane slowly roared out of the hanger and headed for the runway.

Once in the air, Alexis asked him, "Would you like something to eat or drink?" Since there was no time for breakfast when he left the palace, he was hungry.

He was served on a silver tray with fine silverware and a cloth napkin. There were flatbreads, hummus, crackers, and cheese.

There was silence while he was eating. When he had devoured his food and enjoyed the very rich and strong coffee, Alexis asked, "Mr. Knight, are you happy to see me again?"

"Yes, yes I am. As a matter of fact, I was looking forward to it. How are you doing? What I mean is, everything OK with you?"

"Yes," she replied. "Where do you live, what I mean is, where do you call home?" he asked. "Where were you raised?" He continued the questioning, not waiting for an answer.

"I want to learn all about you; since this is going to be a long flight, there's plenty of time. Is that OK with you?"

"Within limits," she said, careful as not to reveal too much.

Alexis talked about a small town near New York City that she called home. She went on telling him that she was raised in Greece, where she served in the military as a teenager and left the country when she was eighteen. Since childhood, the school's taught languages, of which she specialized in Arabic, Spanish, English, French, and a bit of Russian. Alexis' family has worked for the Prince on and off ever since she could remember. Her parents died when she was at a young age, and the Prince has taken care of her ever since. She told him that her parents died in a car accident when she was fourteen and pretty much raised her with the financial help and guidance of the Prince. He was a client of my parents, so I guess that he felt obligated to take care of me." Alexis was a very private person indeed and never revealed who she really was.

She was completely aware of who he was and where he came from. After all, it was Alexis that ran the complete background check on Jonah for the Prince. She was well versed in doing things undercover and unnoticed. Indeed, she knew him very, very well. Alexis was excellent at her job.

"What about you, Mr. Knight? Oh, may I call you Jonah?" she asked.

Jonah proceeded to talk cautiously about his life, being careful not to reveal too much about his parents and what Flagstaff meant to him. Peter always told him to be careful no matter how comfortable he was with someone. No matter what, be on the alert.

However, he still was at ease and relaxed. He just kept talking and staring into her eyes. They were beautiful, dark, and mysterious, he thought. Something was hiding behind them, and it gave him a slightly uneasy feeling. He wanted to know more about her, but something scared him. Suddenly, he had a queasy feeling in his gut and started to lighten up the conversation.

The time flew by very quickly as they became more engrossed in various conversations, being cautious not to reveal too much to each other.

"We are about to land in New York for refueling," the pilot said over the speaker. "Buckle up, Jonah," she said.

The plane landed smoothly at the same airport and glided to the hanger building for fueling and a good meal. He noticed the same man was there to offer him a lavish meal ordered by the Prince.

As the plane door opened, "Welcome back, Mr. Knight, the Prince was very pleased with you," he said. "If there is anything you want, just let him know."

Jonah noticed another tall, husky man walking up the stairs for the next leg of the flight as the other two men departed, getting into a waiting car and driving away.

Alexis went into the office, closed the door, pulled down the shades, and did not emerge for an hour. "Please board the plane. We're ready to leave," the tall, lanky man in the blue overalls said.

The man knocked on the door, alerting her that it was time to leave. Alexis walked out of the closed room and climbed the stairs without saying a word. The plane slowly moved out of the hanger, picking up speed as it headed toward the end of the runway and home.

During the flight, they continued the conversation. This time she was much quieter. She discussed things in general, and certainly nothing personal.

Three hours passed very quickly as the pilots started the descent into the small makeshift, private airport near Hays. Jonah noticed that the extra passenger just sat there, periodically glancing at a magazine, carefully watching everything.

The captain announced, "Mr. Knight, a car will be waiting to take you home. The Prince wanted me to tell you that he appreciated everything that you've done for him. He is one man that never forgets."

Jonah asked, "Alexis, will I see you again?" with the look of a lost boy.

"If you don't mind, I will be staying near here for a couple days. How about dinner?" she asked.

"Yes, yes, of course, I'd love to," he replied eagerly.

The plane landed at nine-twenty P.M. at the unmarked airport. The driver standing outside watching as it slowly approached. The car slowly drove up to the plane's door as it rolled to a stop.

"Welcome back, Mr. Knight," he said. "Please," as he held the rear door opened for him. "Will the lady be joining you?" he asked.

Without another word spoken, Alexis entered the rear of the car. Jonah followed as they sped off into the night. In the rear, the lights at the airport were turned off as the plane flew out into the black starlit night skies, disappearing quickly into the slight thin clouds.

21.

CHAPTER TWENTY-ONE

After a thirty-minute drive, the car drove up to the front of the house. The driver opened the door for both, removed the bags, placed them near the front door, and thanked Jonah for helping the Prince. "Will there be anything else, sir?"

"No, thank you," he replied.

The driver returned to the car and sped off into the quiet darkness.

Jonah held the front door open as Alexis walked in. The house was spotless, thanks to Sarah, his trusted housekeeper. Jonah told Alexis to help herself as she looked over everything, carefully inspecting the rooms of the house as any detective would.

The time was ten minutes to ten, and Jonah was exhausted.

"Alexis, I have a spare bedroom with a separate bath for you. I'll use the bathroom downstairs, so you can have your privacy. Will that be OK?" He asked.

"Thank you, that'll be fine," she said with a smile that would melt the heart of any man.

As they walked up the stairs, Jonah said with a smile, "I'll fix breakfast for us in the morning."

"I'd like that," she responded.

"Good night Alexis," he said as he extended his hand to her. She replied with a soft and gentle kiss on his lips and closed her door.

In the following two days, Jonah showed her everything about the town. They drove down the old Gravel Road near the old house, always stopping and sitting in the car silently for a few moments staring at the

Oak tree standing still. The road he travelled so many times in his dreams and nightmares. The road and the memories brought tears to his eyes as he still remembered what happened, almost like it was yesterday.

"SOLD" kept echoing through his mind as he envisioned Flagstaff selling off everything and how he struggled with it all. He could never forget the man that started it. In his own way, he loved him, not only as a friend but as a mentor and father figure as well. But for the humiliation he faced that day, he certainly couldn't forgive him for that.

Jonah told her what it was like. Everything that happened and how his parents died. They stopped at Margie's Café for lunch as they continued to talk about almost everything. He felt more at ease and comfortable with her, but still, there was something about her that made him a bit nervous.

That night, as they prepared for bed, they kissed goodnight and went into each of their rooms. Since he did not finish his book, Jonah was reading when several minutes passed, when there was a knock at Jonah's door.

"May I come in?" Alexis asked.

"Please do," he replied. "Do you need something?" he said with an eager smile.

"It's a bit cold out there. Can I sleep with you tonight?"

As he moved the covers back, she slipped under, pulling the covers over both. She was wearing a cotton solid blue nightgown without description.

Alexis put her arms firmly around Jonah's waist with light squeezes as she rubbed his stomach. She pulled herself up, kissing him gently on the cheeks, and started nibbling at the closest ear.

Jonah turned to her and mumbled, "Are you sure?"

Without hesitation, she pulled him closer as they evolved with passionate kisses, finally fondling each other as they embraced, their body temperatures rising faster and faster. He turned her nipples with his fingers as he caressed her firm breasts, holding them lightly, squeezing them gently.

Alexis's hand moved down below his navel, holding his member as her head lowered, licking each side as if it were a tasty Popsicle. She was making sure that he was moist, ready to enter her already moist valley.

Jonah started to roll over on top, but she held him, pushing him back as she moved on top of him, slowly putting his full manhood inside and settling down on top until their bodies touched. She controlled every move.

Holding her body straight up, she started to move in ways that he never felt before, reaching a height that were so intense, he thought his testicles was going to burst. She started moaning louder as she moved her lower body in circles, slower, then faster, finally slowing, moaning, and gasping for air as she reached her moment of fullness, reaching new heights of ecstasy.

After several moments, both reeling in pleasure, they evolved in each other's arms, slithering smoothly down, holding each other as she lay tightly in his arms

"Jonah," she asked quietly, "where do you want to be when you finally quit the business?" she asked.

He proceeded to tell her about this place that he read about with white sandy beaches, beautiful weather, and most of all, peace and quiet where no one can find him.

"Where is that?" Alexis asked.

Jonah continued, "On an island called Maui in Hawaii. On the south side on the beach, there is one small hotel called," he hesitated, catching himself, pulled up his guards around, "Umm, I forgot the name, but it's there. That's where I'll be, on the beach, probably drinking a tropical drink."

Alexis just listened quietly, allowing him to talk on, absorbing everything he said.

What is happening to me? He thought. I don't understand what's going on. I feel so strange, like I wanted to jump out of my skin, so disconnected, he kept saying to himself quietly. He has never felt so close, always protected himself against being emotionally hurt by anyone, least of all, a stranger.

Why her? He asked himself, why this woman. Alexis was a woman that had beauty throughout. Jonah never wanted the days to end. Is this the woman that he had been searching for? Someone that he could genuinely fall in love with. *Is she the one?* He questioned himself.

22.

CHAPTER TWENTY-TWO

At approximately Three o'clock in the morning, unusual rustling sounds were coming from outside of the house on a usually quiet night. The noises became more muffled and came closer.

The bedroom door swung open with a loud bang. A tall, dark clothed man stood there pointing his snub-nosed .38 caliber Smith and Wesson revolver at Jonah; he shouted, "Mr. Sanchez sends his regards."

Suddenly the man dropped his gun-grabbing his throat with both hands, trying to get rid of the lamp cord wrapped tightly around his neck. He was being choked as her knee was pushing high on his back, pulling the cord tighter until he was lifeless, falling to the floor. His eyes were bulging, remaining motionless. Alexis rolled him over on his stomach as not to look at him.

All Jonah could do was to look at her, speechless for a moment.

"What just happened?" he asked with a tremble in his voice.

Stumbling with her words, "I heard a noise and was a little scared. I got up and saw this man trying to hurt you. I will never allow anyone to hurt you as long as I can, I promise."

Jonah jumped out of bed and held her tightly.

"Alexis, I think that I," hesitating for a moment, "thank you," he said. Alexis said nothing as they held each other tightly for a moment. He wanted to say a lot, but he was fearful that his words might cause more harm than good.

"WOW! That was something that was certainly unexpected. Thank you for saving my life. I owe you a lot," Jonah said.

Without saying another word, Jonah replied, "Lets' clean up this mess. Give the Sheriff a call.

"Why don't you wait until I'm gone to work, and then you can tell the sheriff, ok?" she asked.

"Sure," he said; caught off guard, Jonah agreed.

Alexis was a physically strong woman, considering her height and body structure. Alexis immediately interrupted, "I'll take care of this. Don't worry; no one will know what happened. OK? He was just someone who tried to rob the house." Jonah agreed as they proceeded to do their individual tasks.

Before Alexis covered the body with a bed sheet, she and without hesitating, she ruthlessly slit his throat just to make sure that he was dead, then dragged the man's body out of the room and down the stairs, leaving him outside near the stairs to the cellar and out the back door.

"You should contact the Sheriff early in the morning and tell him that you killed him and please, pretend that I was never here," Alexis remarked almost with a commanding voice.

"I'll be leaving in the morning, gotta go to work," Alexis said calmly.

"Can I drive you to the airport?" Jonah asked with the look of a little lost boy. Around Alexis he always felt like this.

"No, no, thank you," she replied. "I am being picked up."

"A car will pick me up. Can we go back to sleep now? Long day tomorrow!" she said. "Mind if I sleep here with you?" Jonah agreed. They went back to bed, holding each other tightly for the rest of the night.

In the morning, Jonah fixed a light breakfast for her, eggs, toast, and coffee. The car arrived at noon to pick up their passenger.

"Will I see you again?" he asked with the lost, innocent yet childish look on his face.

"We will meet again soon, Jonah, I promise," she said as she walked out the door to the waiting car. She turned and waved as they sped off. Jonah leaned against the doorpost, watching as the car disappeared into the rising afternoon dust with a void in his chest. Jonah called the sheriff and told him that there was a break in and could he come over to take care of this criminal. When he came over, he asked many questions before that Jonah had the body removed ending a terrifying day.

23.

CHAPTER TWENTY-THREE

Over the next few weeks, Jonah went about the usual business, talking with everybody over at Margie's Café, saying nothing about the attempted murder at his house.

The central meeting place for just about everybody in town and the place for a cup of her famous coffee, delicious sandwiches, and homemade pies. He could not get Alexis out of his mind. For sure, she was the right one. Finally, he had someone to love and be loved in return.

Since his travels and meeting Alexis, Jonah was not the same. He looked at everybody and everything so differently. He thought about the Prince, the special gift from him, Nadia, and most of all, Alexis. He really missed her a lot. *Was he ever going to see her again*, he thought to himself?

He thought that the adventure was over, and he was back to the mundane life of the local Auctioneer, but he would never be the same. Back to the usual, resolving himself that he might not see Alexis ever again. After all, how can a heart unknown to love live like before after knowing the lust of belongingness?

The weather was getting warmer; the sun shone through the clouds as they disappeared in the brightly lit skies. The people of Hays were happier and smiled more. The land was clearing up, and the earth began to show some promise. Some of the townspeople started to plant seeds in hopes that things will grow again in this desolate land of theirs.

Margie's Café was getting more crowded, and some of the small businesses were getting busier.

On Monday, six weeks to the day, a strange new dust-covered black Cadillac drove into town with two seemingly middle-aged men. As Jonah was walking down the street, the car stopped and asked,

"Hey, do you know where I can get some food and a cup of coffee? It's been a long drive," one said.

"Sure do," he replied, "Go on down to Margie's Café down the street. Best food in town."

"Thanks," one said, "by the way," as he fumbled through some papers, "do you know a guy named, umm, I got it here somewhere, Knight?"

"Don't know the guy," was Jonah's response, as he hurried quickly away from them.

"Thanks," one said as they drove off down the street to the Café.

After their meal, the men started to ask questions about Jonah.

"Is he a good Auctioneer?" they asked.

"Best one in all of the near states, good reputation," Margie said. "The best," she added. A real good man; everyone loves him around here."

"Where can we find this guy?" one asked.

"His office is on the north side of town. Just go on down and turn right on Gopher. It's the blue and white house at the end. You'll see his shingle hanging out there," Margie said.

"Thanks," as they walked out, got into their car, and headed to Jonah's house.

Just as he was walking into the house, the men caught up to him. "You Jonah Knight?" they asked.

"Who wants to know," he said firmly.

"My name is John Benson, and this is my partner, Bob Paterson. We represent a group of people that would like you to perform an auction for us." Benson said.

"You were highly recommended by a friend of our client. They said that you are the man to get the job done," he continued.

"Come on in," as Jonah opened the door. Looking at the men closely, he said. "First, I have several questions. Is that OK with you?" Jonah asked.

"Fire away," Paterson said.

"First of all, who told you about me, second, what will I be selling, third, how much would I be paid, and fourth, where will the sale take place?"

"Fair enough," Benson continued, "First, you were highly recommended by a friend of my clients, a guy named Prince Nabob, Najib, or something like that. Second, it's a large number of weapons, boxed and ready to be shipped to the buyer, whoever that is; third, the total payment will be thirty thousand, and forth, in the southern part of El Salvador. Hopefully, that has answered your questions."

"If I accept, when will I leave, and how will I get there?" Jonah asked, trying not to show any excitement. *Another adventure*, he thought.

"Now that I've answered your questions, I have one for you. Will you do it? Is the pay sufficient?"

After a few moments of silence, Jonah replied, "OK, I'll do it under one additional condition, I require an armed bodyguard. Is that good for you? I mean, that is part of my conditions before I agree."

Absolutely, agreed then. We were hoping that you would do this job, thanks, Mr. Knight," both men said with a smile of gratitude on their faces.

"A car will come for you, lets' see, today's Tuesday; the car will be here Thursday morning, say, around Eight A.M. or so. Be ready, please!"

"Make it Eight P.M. instead, okay? When will I receive the advance payment? Can't leave without it, one-third is usual, but one-half would give me a better incentive," Jonah insisted.

Benson reached into his inside coat pocket and pulled out an envelope. Will ten thousand in cash be due for a start?"

"Yep, that'll work. This will be good, thank you." Jonah said.

24.

CHAPTER TWENTY-FOUR

Eight o'clock Thursday evening came about quickly. Jonah was waiting with his small black duffle bag packed with needed essentials and clothing. There was a loud knock at the door.

"Mr. Knight, Mr. Knight, your car is waiting, sir. Will you be long, sir?" the driver asked.

Jonah opened the door, handing the driver his duffle bag. He left a note for Sarah, the housekeeper, and locked the house. The driver quickly opened the back door. Jonah climbed in, and off they went. The driver didn't say a word on their journey. They drove past the airport cutoff, continuing further down the road.

"Hey, Driver, where are we going?" Jonah asked.

"Another half-hour or so, sir," the driver replied, remaining silent, trying to avoid further conversation.

Driving another forty minutes, they arrived at what appeared to be a small private airport where there was a medium-sized plane waiting for the passenger to arrive. This must be the same airport that he flew out of before, he thought. The driver got out, grabbed the duffle, and opened the car door for Jonah, pointing to the plane's stairway. "Please, Sir, this way."

As he started to walk up the stairs, Benson greeted him.

"Hey, Jonah, welcome aboard. Glad to see you. Grab a seat; we are off and running. Buckle up now!"

Once aboard, Jonah looked throughout the plane, hoping that Alexis was aboard. He really missed their conversations, companionship, and most of all, *he really missed her*.

Damn, he thought to himself. She never gave him any contact information on how to call or write. Suddenly, he felt very alone.

The plane taxied down the private airfield to the end, slowly turning as the engines revved to a loud roar, racing down the runway, lifting into the clear evening skies.

Jonah was able to look out the windows, not much secrecy, he thought, probably a simple sale. No problems this is going to be easy.

After a short refueling stop in Los Angeles, they finally arrive at a small airport on the south of the city. A car was following the plane as it slowly taxied down the field, stopping at the far end. Jonah, Benson, and Paterson walked down the stairway to the waiting Cadillac limousine. The driver held the rear door open.

"Common Jonah, we gotta go," Benson said with a loud voice.

The driver was a rather tall heavyset medium complexion, wearing a suit in the hot weather, with a slight bulge under the arm.

They drove for fifteen minutes at a high rate of speed to a small hotel where they were going to spend the night.

Paterson started the conversation, "Jonah, may I call you Jonah?" he asked.

"Sure, that would be fine," Jonah replied. Paterson continued,

"Tonight, we will stay here, have a good meal, and will go to bed early. We gotta get an early start tomorrow morning, OK? We'll have breakfast, and then we'll review the auction facility and the merchandise." Jonah asked, "What will I be selling?" Benson replied, "Something of great value that we will see when we get there."

"How much do you think it will sell for?" Jonah asked. "It's only a guess, but I think about half a million or so," Benson butted in.

"One Million, Okay, what kind of buyers are going to be there?" Jonah asked.

Benson replied, "Uh, just do your job. We'll take care of everything else. How about dinner? This place got great steaks," trying to avoid an answer.

"OK," Jonah said with an uneasy, queasy feeling.

When they were having their espresso coffees after the large porterhouse steak dinner, Paterson started to talk, "The auction will take place about ten-thirty. We'll have to get there about nine to run over the logistics of the building, OK? If all goes well, we'll be on our way home by two."

"Guess so," Jonah said. "I'll be ready."

The large windup alarm clock rang at seven sharp. By seven twenty-five, Jonah was downstairs waiting.

The men came down the stairs together, "Hi Jonah, morning, did you sleep OK? Come on, have a little breakfast, and we are off," Benson quipped.

"We gotta catch another plane to get to the place. Let's go there, buddy!"

25.

CHAPTER TWENTY-FIVE

After landing the following late afternoon at another secluded distant airport away from the main city, a car was waiting to take them to the auction site.

The sun was going down, but the humidity was high, sweat was running down his forehead. The heat here is comparable to an oven, he thought to himself.

Once inside the building, the men showed Jonah where the sale will take place and what he should do if there is a problem.

"After the sale, I want you to drop under the platform through the trap door that will lead to a tunnel that will take you to safety, got it?" Paterson said.

Paterson continued, "Pay attention, Knight! Your safety is very much our concern. Please, if you follow our instructions, everything will be just fine. Is that OK with you?"

"Yes, yes, of course, is there anything else?" Jonah asked.

"Well, yes, there is," Benson added. "There will be someone waiting for you underneath the trap door. Follow him, and he will guide you to safety, got that?"

"Yes, yes I do. Thanks for that," Jonah said.

"By the way, hang on to this," as he handed Jonah a loaded 9MM Ruger Automatic pistol. "Ya know how to use it, don't ya?"

At nine-thirty, some very interesting-looking people started to enter the room and looked for seats. There were three women and eleven men. Some were dressed in suits, and some others wore long white patterned shirts, each with bulges around the midsection. Jonah felt a little queasy and thought this time, there might be some trouble.

"Ladies and gentlemen, please have a seat," Benson said as he proceeds to do the introductions. "These are the terms and conditions for this sale. Please always keep your weapons undercover. If anyone draws their weapon, they will be shot immediately. Does everyone understand that?"

As they nodded in agreement, their bodyguards stood down; Benson continued, "You all have inspected the items that will be auctioned today. Mr. Jonah Knight will conduct the sale. All sales are final, Now, Mr. Knight."

As Jonah stood up and started, "Gentlemen, I will start the bidding at five hundred thousand," as one nodded his head.

"Now, let's get serious; seven hundred thousand is a bargain."

"Thank you," he said to the last bidder, "now one million is a deal for weapons like these, OK, now one million two hundred," Jonah spoke with power and firmness.

He noticed that some bidders were getting agitated with a look of anger. "Lets' get serious with a bid of two million." The bidder in the third row raised his hand with a slicing motion noting that his bid was half of the offered bid price.

"Now the bid is one million, two-fifty. Are there any more bids?" He asked.

"I'm going to sell them. "The successful Bidder, once paid, must pick up as soon as possible," Jonah instructed the group."

Going once, all bids must be in, Twice," he raised his hand to close the sale, when someone from the back of the room shouted, "TWO MILLION."

One bidder in the second row was grumbling about the price.

"Tell you what I'll do, I'll give you two million, two hundred, and that's my final offer. Take it, Knight, or we're done here."

"Jonah replied, "This is an auction. These items are going to sell to the highest bidder." Jonah insisted.

"The bidder in the back of the room row raised his hand for three million. Any more bids? Going once, twice, pausing for a few moments, hearing none," as he was abruptly interrupted.

"Don't you fuck'n argue with me, Knight! I don't lose, got it!" His two bodyguards started to stand. Jonah replied with a raised voice, "If you want it, then raise your bid!" he said while holding his ground firm.

"Sit down," Benson said sternly to the men.

"OK," he said, being very annoyed. "I'll bid Three Million one hundred, and that's it."

"Please continue, Jonah!" Benson insisted.

The other bidders were starting to get restless. Each one, including the woman, was moving restlessly in their seats. Jonah noticed the woman was holding her purse tightly, slowly reaching inside, her hand clenching something. His instincts told him that this female was dangerous, very, very dangerous.

Finally, the bid from the back of the room, "THREE MILLION, FIVE HUNDRED," the silent bidder said.

Jonah continued selling to a very agitated crowd, watching the man in the first row with an eye on the woman. "The bid is at three million, five hundred," Jonah said firmly.

"I need a substantial bid over that amount. Either you are in, or you're out. DECLARE YOURSELF NOW!"

"No," the bidder said, "I said the price was three million. Either you say *SOLD* to me, or I will," said the man angrily.

Seven of the other bidders hurried out the door without saying a word, taking their entourage with them.

Benson signaled the man standing on the left, "Be watchful," He whispered to Jonah. Watch the guy and especially the woman; she's his bodyguard," Benson whispered into Jonah's ear.

"THAT SHIT IS MINE," he yelled loudly. She pulled one gun out of her purse in her right hand and the left hand, another small .38 caliber pistol. She aimed them at Jonah, preparing to shoot.

She jumped to her feet, knocking her chair down, firing both guns rapidly at Jonah.

Paterson yelled, "GET OUT, NOW!"

Shots rang out, and Jonah was hit in the right shoulder and another buried deep in his side.

Jonah dodged into the trap door faster than a heartbeat. Ducking into the tunnel as instructed. The man waiting said, "Follow me, senior, quickly."

The few remaining people lunged at the floor. When the shooting was over, they got up, running to the nearest exit.

More shots rang out as the woman, riddled with gunshots from both Benson and Paterson, tumbling over the chairs, landed on the floor with a thud.

A chilling thought ran through his mind breaking out into a cold sweat.

Is this my Gravel Road? Is this the end? He thought while continuing to run around the turns as fast as his legs can move?

The tunnel seemed to be miles long when it was only a few hundred feet. When they came to an end, the man opened a steel barred door where a car was waiting to take him back to the hotel. There were two armed men, one in the back seat and the driver. The man behind him pushed him into the back seat with force. Their automatic guns were in their hands, ready to protect him.

"Let's go," the driver repeated himself, shouting.

The car jolted forward, throwing Jonah backward into the seat in pain that he never knew before. Damn, he thought, this really burns and hurts and with the loss of blood, he felt faint.

They sped quickly down the street, disappearing into the bowels of the mysterious city. Twenty minutes later, they drove into the rear entrance in the hotel's underground garage, where the car came to a screeching halt.

"Follow me, Senior," the driver said, grabbing Jonah and putting his good arm over his neck as they made their way up the stairs.

They rushed up the stairs and grabbed his duffle bag. "We must leave now, common, let's move, man. Thank you for your service. Mr. Patterson will join you at the airport. Just sit, and I'll do it for you. The Doctor will meet you."

Talking a quick look around the room and left, slamming the door shut.

As the car sped into the closed hanger. With help, Jonah boarded the plane, all while bleeding that would not stop; Paterson arrived a few minutes later.

The doctor waited on the plane to bandage him up and tried to remove the bullets, so the wound didn't get infected.

Paterson handed Jonah the balance of his remaining fee of twenty thousand in cash with very little conversation as agreed.

"Thanks very much for your services," Paterson said to a groggy Jonah.

"Where's Benson?" Jonah asked.

"He had to take care of a few things. Don't worry, and he'll be fine. You're able to identify the right buyer for us; the weapons were sold for more than we ever expected. To avoid any problems, we had to leave quickly. Again, thanks for your service, good job! Maybe I'll see you again, have a good flight, and by the way, sorry that ya got shot." Paterson said as he closed the door behind Jonah.

The plane left as soon as he boarded. This time, there were two other men to onboard. There was no conversation during the flight. Paterson mentioned that his boss would be pleased. I'm sure that he'll mention this to the Prince.

Jonah arrived at the same airport they departed from; the waiting car drove Jonah back to Hays.

Back home, he thought to himself, the same town, same people, same streets, and same phony smiles, always the same. One day, I've gotta get out of here. One day, one day soon. I will save my money and will retire. Good thought, but I don't think that it's going to happen, at least not for a long while.

26.

CHAPTER TWENTY-SIX

Several months passed uneventfully, and all things were quiet in Hays, Kansas. The farms were starting to flourish, with new crops creeping up through the fresh, moist dirt.

People started to smile more and were friendlier. Jonah got a little busy doing a few local auctions while Margie's Café continued bustling from morning through dinner.

At the same time, the weather got warm enough to repaint the house, both inside and outside. The weather demanded planting some flowers that Sarah helped pick out at the general store, and in general, just relax.

Several new people were walking around the revived, bustling town. Jonah was always watchful, always on guard, fearful of being shot by someone upset at one of the overseas sales.

He always watched everything, learning from lessons passed. Jonah started to carry his new Browning .380 caliber automatic concealed under his shirt tucked tightly in his belt, ready to aim whenever the time asks for action.

One morning in August, sorting through the usual mail, he noticed an unmarked blue envelope pushed under the front door, "Please read," was written on the outside. Curiosity prevailed as he opened the letter carefully:

"My Dearest Jonah,

Hopefully, your journey was successful. I will be in town tomorrow morning for a few days, and I would appreciate it if you could spare some time for me. Do you have room for a lonely girl?

Miss you very much, I can't wait to see you, Alexis."

After reading the note, Jonah was certainly looking forward to seeing this woman.

The following day, just before dawn, a loud knock at the door startled him forgetting that she was coming. "Yes, yes, I'm coming. Hold your horses." Rubbing his eyes, Jonah opened the door, forgetting that she was coming. "Who is it?" he said as the door opened.

"Hi," she said. "Got a room for a lonely girl?" Jonah hugged and kissed her tightly.

"Do I have a room for you? That's a hell of a question. Want some breakfast?" he asked as they headed for the kitchen.

Jonah asked her about her travels, being careful not to mention what happened or where he was, what was sold, being fully aware that secrecy is mandatory in this business. No one must ever know what went on at any sale or event.

"Did you have any problems on the trip?" She asked. Avoiding the question altogether, he asked, "How long will you be here?"

"Just a few days," She said with disappointment under her breath. Jonah couldn't understand if the disappointment was for the little time they could spend together or for the answer he didn't give.

The time they spent together was perfect. Jonah was careful not to reveal his feelings to her, fearful she would never return. He has never loved anyone, but this woman stole his heart. How could he ever tell her that he loved her?

"Where are you going this time? He asked. She stuttered a moment, "I have to fly to Europe. I'll be back in a few weeks. Will you be here?"

"I'm not sure, but if not, I'll hide the key under the first flower pot on the window for you, okay?" Jonah replied.

27.

CHAPTER TWENTY-SEVEN

Alexis kept sending long letters every other week describing the country where she was. There was never a return address, only a description of the area. Whenever she was in the country, she would call, and they would talk for long periods about things in general, without ever telling him where she was and not being specific.

Jonah was eating dinner at Margie's in early September when an older, well-dressed, distinguished-looking woman sat down beside him.

"Is the food good here?" she asked with a heavy Irish accent. She was wearing normal everyday street clothing and a blue hat that was tilted slightly on her head.

"The best," he said, finishing his coffee. "I'm looking for someone who is supposed to live here. Maybe you know him. His name is," as she reached into her pocket, grabbing a crumpled piece of paper.

"His name is I think Knit, or Night, or nightly or something like that. Excuse me, but my English is not so good." She gave a justification.

"Would it be Knight?" He quipped.

"Yes, that is the man. Do you know him?" she asked.

"I might. What do you want with him?" He asked.

"I'm sorry, but it is personal," she said.

"Do you know him?" she asked again.

"Maybe I can help you. Go on down the street and turn right on Gopher. It's the big blue and white house at the end."

"Thank you," she replied with a smile, finished her coffee, paid the check, and left.

Jonah waited for a moment, slipped out the back door, taking the side street and alley's, headed for the house, arriving before she did.

"Door is open. Come on in," Jonah replied, sitting at his desk, holding his gun tightly on his lap, ready, not forgetting the woman in El Salvador.

She walked in, surprised, "You're the man at the restaurant!" She exclaimed.

She was slim, standing five foot four inches, he guessed, thin, tall block heels, wearing a dark brown trench coat. She was wearing a matching hat with a veil partially covering her face—one hand placed in a pocket and the other holding her relatively large purse.

"Guess so; how can I help you?" Jonah asked, squeezing the gun tighter under the desk, ready to shoot. "First, what's your name?"

"My name is Caryn Moran. I represent the Bureau of Antiquities in London. Sorry for the bad accent, but a girl can't be too careful nowadays," speaking in perfect English.

"I've been sent here on a mission to find you for a, err, umm, job. Are you available, say, next week?"

"Who exactly are you, and I need details, Ms. Moran? I need details!" Jonah said. "Who sent you?"

"I understand," she replied. "Do you mind if I remove my coat and hat? Really hate wearing this damn hat," she quipped.

"The person who sent me here told me to tell you that the name Najib might ring a bell. Do you know who that is?" she asked. "I've never met him personally."

Jonah was silent for a moment, releasing his tight grip on the revolver, putting both hands on the desk. Ah yes, Najib, my friend needs me, he thought. I feel a little better now.

"Yes, OK, now tell me what you want me to do and my fee, what is my fee? Details, Ms. Moran, I need details, please."

"Mr. Knight, the job consists of buying a certain piece of art for a museum that was stolen several years ago. I know that you are in the business of selling, but they thought that you would be perfect for the job. Are you OK with that?"

"Who are they?" he asked.

"THEY are the museum curators," she replied.

"Where would this job take place?" Jonah asked.

"Our sources tell us that this particular piece of art piece is in Monaco. You will be travelling to the southern coast of France."

"When do I leave?" he asked with a serious tone.

"Next week, you will leave next Thursday," She said. "By the way, you do know how to handle firearms?"

"Yes, I do. Why do you ask?"

"Just asking," Moran said.

"Aren't we forgetting something? What about my fee?"

"Yes, yes, of course. I am authorized to pay you up to twenty-five thousand for your services, including all expenses. You'll be travelling first class."

"Make it thirty, and we have a deal," pushing the price higher.

"How about that we meet in the middle at twenty-seven thousand, five hundred, and then we have an agreement?"

"Agreed," said Jonah.

"Thank you. I'm sure that you know that at least half is due now."

"All I have is ten thousand, but the rest will be given to you when to job is done." As she handed him the brown manila envelope with the cash.

"Do I have to count it?" he asked.

"It's all there, no need," she said with assurance.

"Mr. Knight, I'm sure that you will tell no one of our meetings. There are a few people out there that will do anything to stop this sale. Please be careful, I mean exceptionally careful," as she rose up from the wing-back brown leather chair, put her coat and hat back on, and headed to the door.

"Everything will be taken care of. A car will pick you up in the morning and take you to the airport. You will be contacted on the plane. Someone will come to you and mention my full name to you. This person will guide you from there. Thank you, Mr. Knight. The Museum will be forever in your debt. Do you have any questions for me? If not, I really must go now."

"What time will I be picked up?" As Moran tightened her coat and grabbed her hat, "I was told that Eight in the evening is the appropriate time for you, bye, bye now," as she left, gently closing the door behind her.

28.

CHAPTER TWENTY-EIGHT

Right on schedule, the car arrived at exactly eight in the evening. The driver knocked on the door, "Mr. Knight, you ready?"

As per usual, Jonah left a note for Sarah prior to locking the house. He then climbed into the car and went off to the airport.

Once he got onboard on the plane, Jonah noticed that there were about fifteen people from a quick count. Nobody approached him as he was headed to the destination. About an hour before the flight ended, a woman sat down next to him.

"HI!" she said. My friend told me to say Hi to you," she said.

"And who might that be?" He asked.

"Her name is Caryn Moran. She said that you might need some information before we land. Look for the man holding up a sign with your name on it. He'll take you to the hotel where you are already registered. Enjoy your dinner; it's paid for." "You will be contacted, sorry, but no questions now." "Say, you're cute," She giggled quietly as she moved back to her seat.

The plane arrived in Monaco early in the evening, the following day. A man in a blue suit was holding up a sign reading, "Knight."

Jonah walked up to him without saying a word handed him his duffle as they walked to a waiting Rolls Royce limousine.

"Where are we going?" Jonah asked.

"Hotel Sube Continental, sir," the driver said. "It is the most beautiful hotel, directly on the water. Great views, I must say."

Jonah and the driver approached the desk. "Bonjour, Welcome, Mr. Knight, welcome. We have been expecting you," the desk clerk said. "One moment, please, sir," as the clerk pushed a mute button to summon the hotel manager.

He came out of the office wearing a dark gray suit with a blue tie.

"Welcome, welcome. We have been expecting you. Your Suite is prepared and ready. Mr. Knight. This envelope came for you yesterday."

"Thank you," He put it into his pocket as the bellman picked up the duffle and guided him to the elevator and up to the penthouse suite. "Can I do anything else for you, Sir?"

"No, thank you." Jonah said as he handed him a two-dollar tip, "Please close the door!" As soon as he closed the door, Jonah opened the envelope.

"*Mr. Knight,*

After breakfast tomorrow morning, say ten o'clock, please walk down to the boat dock. Sit on the bench closest to the walkway on your left side. You will be contacted.

Thank you for your understanding."

Feeling a bit nervous and after the morning meal of Eggs Benedict, English muffin, and coffee, Jonah took a leisurely walk down to the boat, enjoying the exceptionally warm temperature and beautiful scenery surrounded by blue waters. As always, Jonah looked in every direction to make sure he was not being followed.

As instructed, he sat on the bench just past the walkway, looking out at the large yachts docked at the harbor. He was very cautious, watching everything and everyone around him.

After fifteen minutes, a man walking past stopped, "Nice day, isn't it?" he said with a New York accent. "Mind if I sit?"

"Go ahead. Yes, yes, it is, nice day," Jonah replied.

After a few minutes passed by, "You Jonah Knight?" he asked.

"Yep!" he replied.

"Please come with me. See that large yacht down there; we're going to get on it. Big, isn't it? We're going on a short boat ride, oh, don't worry, you're perfectly safe," He continued. "Follow me!"

Without hesitating, he followed the man down the gangway to the large yacht, the name "LUCKY STAR," brightly scripted in bright blue letters with grey shadows around each letter on the rear of the boat.

The Capitan, as well as two women, greeted them. "Bonjour, Mr. Knight. Please sit and enjoy the ride," he said. "You're the last one to arrive. Please go to the rear deck where you can enjoy the beautiful scenery of Monaco."

"How big is this boat" Jonah asked. He was a bit nervous since he has never been on anything that floats. The crew member answered, "This is only seventy-two feet long, sir."

The Captain signaled the crew to get underway as the engines slowly moved the yacht away from the dock area and roared out of the harbor.

Jonah walked to the stern section, where he was surprised to find four other men and two women travelling to the same destination.

"Beautiful day for a sale, isn't it?" one of the men said with a slight laugh.

A few suspicious smiles came from two of the others. Each one was watching the other, their competition for the auction.

The two women are wearing tank tops and shorts, exposing as much leg as possible, approached Jonah,

"Would you like some wine or other refreshment, sir? Have some freshly made shrimp appetizers. They're really good!"

After a forty-five-minute ride, the "LUCKY STAR" docked on a small island. They all followed each other off at the dock without saying a word.

They walked single file on a narrow walkway to a very large mansion at the top of a hill, where they were greeted by a large, neatly dressed man opening the door with a smile.

"Welcome, everybody. How ya all doin? Good to see you all today. Just call me Pete," he said with a deep southern Texas accent. "Welcome to my humble little shack."

"Come on in," he continued, "first we gotta eat lunch, and then we're goin' to check out the picture. You can review it at your leisure. As you all know, please don't touch the piece. The owner will get pretty mad."

Extending his hand, Jonah started, "Good to see an American. My name is…" when he was abruptly interrupted,

"I know who ya are, Buba. You're not going to be here long enough to know ya."

How strange, he thought.

Jonah observed each of the others very carefully, checking the competition. He was not told or given any instructions, just told to show up.

After a typical French lunch, including wine, cheese, crackers, and fruit, he was approached by one of the women. Speaking softly, whispering in his ear, "Mr. Knight, after I leave, please excuse yourself for a lavatory visit and go into the door on your right in the corner," she said and walked away, quickly disappearing down the hallway.

After a minute, Jonah asked where the lavatory was and walked into the next room. When he was out of sight of the others, he opened the door on the right as per the instructions given to him.

"Close the door," she said in a soft feminine whispered voice.

"We must speak quickly, please take this gun, and put it into your pocket, just in case," as she handed him the loaded .38 Smith & Wesson snub nose.

29.

CHAPTER TWENTY-NINE

"We don't have much time. Listen to me. There are two very ruthless men out there that will be bidding against you. There is one. His name is John Knoch. Watch him closely. He is a very dangerous man with a lot of friends. He's the one wearing the bright printed shirt."

Without catching her breath, she continued, "You are authorized to bid up to seven million. From the information that we've received, they will be bidding from four to five million. Do not worry about the details. Win the bidding first, leave quickly after the sale. A speedboat will be waiting to take you back to shore.

Your bag has been packed and will be waiting for you at the airport. Whatever you do, please, be careful. Do you understand, Mr. Knight? If necessary, use this gun and hold on to it, for safety, of course. You may have to use it. Keep it within easy reach."

"Absolutely," Jonah replied. "Please leave now and go back to the room. I will follow shortly," she said. "Do not make anything but small talk with the others. Keep your conversations very short and to the point. Do not offer any advice to anyone. Now go back to the others!"

"When do we see the painting?" Jonah asked the Texan.

"The painting will be available in the auction room shortly," Pete said. "Your people saw it and checked it out. Just do your job in there, Bubba."

After thirty minutes passed, he motioned the group to follow him to the auction room, where the painting was proudly displayed on an easel.

"Ladies and gentlemen, may I present, "Renoir." Please don't touch the painting. Your representatives inspected the painting and verified its' authenticity. Please take your seats so we can get started with this shindig."

"The bidding will start at one million," Pete said. "I'll take that bid," one said, as another chimed in, "Good start, but not good enough. Let's begin at two million."

Jonah sat quietly waiting for the right moment as the bidding continued to rise without saying a word, now at two million.

"The next increment will be three Million. Do we have any takers?" the host asked.

Hesitating, Pete waited for another bid. After a few moments of silence, Jonah raised his hand slightly, "Two million Five hundred." The two men that he was told to watch looked at him with murder in their eyes.

"Thank you, there Bubba," he said.

"I'll go the limit. Let's make it three million; that the best that I can do," Knoch said angrily.

Quietly, Knoch whispered into Jonah's ear, "Knight, don't overbid me, buddy boy, you'll regret it," he said demandingly and with a heavy New York accent.

"Don't threaten me," Jonah said quietly, staring him down. I'll bid three Million, five hundred."

"The bidding is now at three million five hundred. Are there any other bidders for this very beautiful rare painting?"

"Offered once," Pete stated with a firm voice gazing around the room. "Offered twice at three million, five hundred, third and last call," Pete paused for a moment, come on there, folks, anything else?" The room fell silent, "I'm going to do it there, folks, sold to Mr. Knight. Thanks' their Bubba. Payment has been arranged on your behalf."

"OK, Knight," Knoch quickly pulled out .45 from his waist, pointing it at Jonah, "You rotten Son of a Bitch." Jonah pushed his arm up in the air as the wild shot rang out, breaking some crystals on the expansive chandelier.

Jonah hit the floor, rolling over on his stomach. Knoch went over to him lying there.

"You bastard, I told you, don't fuck with me!"

Jonah rolled over on his back, shooting Knoch three times rapidly in the gut. Instantly, he fell, knocking over two rows of chairs, dead.

Jonah rose to his feet, grabbing the nearest chair, trying to hold his composure. He was used to shooting at targets, not at a human being, let alone killing someone. He started to shake with nervousness. Never shot anyone, WOW! This was a rush, he thought to himself.

Almost immediately, Jonah was grabbed by two men, and one held his arm, the other one grabbing the pistol.

"Hurry, Knight gotta go. Knoch's got lots of friends."

"Come 'on, now," as they pulled him out the patio doors of the auction room, running down to the boat dock to a waiting speedboat. "Get in," one said as he pushed him, falling clumsily into the boat.

The bow rose quickly as it raced full speed out into the sparkling blue open waters.

Once at the other shore, Jonah was greeted at dockside, a white Rolls Royce was waiting to carry him to the airport and the waiting plane to take him home.

Jonah boarded the plane, grabbed a seat, and buckled up as the plane rolled out onto the tarmac, heading up into the late afternoon sun.

"You can relax now, Jonah. You're safe now," came a familiar voice from the rear.

"Alexis? Alexis, is that you, that really you?"

"Buckle up," she said, "we've got a long flight ahead of us."

As the plane soared upward into the bright sun-filled sky, she walked over,

"Is this seat taken?"

30.

CHAPTER THIRTY

Days and weeks turn into months; Alexis would appear for a few days and sometimes up to a week, and then she would leave for extended periods of time, spending less and less time with him.

The air was filling up with more flights, he certainly could understand her not staying long. Each time she would come in wearing different expensive clothes from her travels. She would bring him little gifts from around the world.

I was very peaceful in Hays. The town was growing into a small city; crops were growing, and the dust was slowly disappearing. The lands were starting to look green, the corn stalks growing high and the town's people smiling. Margie's café was busy from early breakfast to dinner. She had to hire two more waitresses and one additional short order cook to handle the additional business.

He took the train to attend the National Auctioneers Association at the Palmer House Hotel on State Street in Chicago in August. Midway Airport was too far, but the train arrived at Union Station, which was much closer to Downtown.

In the various meetings, they discussed new ways to sell the various types of items at auction. Most of it, Jonah already knew, thanks to a lot of experience and Peter Flagstaff, his mentor.

Most of the auctioneers made a good living, but nothing like me, he thought.

After the third day of listening to the lectures, good food, and conversations with the other Auctioneers from all over the country, it was time to pack up and go home.

It was just a short taxi ride to Union Station; Jonah was looking forward to an uneventful, relaxing six-hour train ride home.

He stopped by the bar for a quick drink and snack before he boarded the train. The area was crowded as people arrived to catch their train to go home and other destinations both near and far.

He noticed a man in a dark blue suit and a rather tall woman following him into the bar. These were the same two he noticed at the hotel sitting in the lobby.

He picked a seat near the mirror at the end to watch his back. After a few moments, the man sat on the stool next to him and the woman sat on the other side of him.

"How's the food?" he said. "Guess its ok." Jonah quipped back.

"Names Jeffries, my friends call me Jeff. That's my friend on the other side of you."

"Hi, names Liz. Nice shirt." She said.

What's your name there, handsome?"

"My name or what people call me?" Jonah said laughingly.

"Joe Day," he replied, being very careful not to be known. He had to be very careful. After all, Knoch had friends, and he really didn't trust anyone he didn't know.

"Taking the train somewhere or just stopped by for a drink?" Jonah asked.

"Goin' to St. Louis, and you?"

"Me too, guess I'll see you on the train," as Jonah slid off the stool, turned, heading for the train.

31.

CHAPTER THIRTY-ONE

Jonah, once aboard, found a lounge seat, relaxed, opened his briefcase, and started to read some of the printed material he picked up at the convention. As the Porter passed by, he stopped and asked him for a Vodka and orange juice cocktail.

"That's called a screwdriver," the Porter answered. He loosened his tie, put his jacket on the seat next to him, grabbed the newspaper, sat back, and relaxed.

Fifteen minutes after the train left the station, the same two people sat down opposite him.

"Hi again, handsome, Mister Joe Day, or is it, Jonah Knight?"

Startled by their comment, "Who?"

"Now, Jonah, let's quit fooling around," Jeffries said.

"What do you want with me, and who the hell are you people? I want the truth, got it? No Bull Shit," Jonah asked.

"Ok, Ok," Jeffries said. We both work for the United States government, Secret Service division, and need your expertise with a project. You game?"

"I don't know who you think I am, but I'm just a local auctioneer just trying to edge out a living."

"Now whose Bull Shitting who their Buddy boy," Jeffries replied. "Let's get to the chase. We know who you are, Knight. We can do a few things, we can make your life miserable, or you can do a great service for your country. What do ya say?" Why don't you take a few minutes to mull it over while we get something to drink, Ok?"

Neither of them took their eyes off him as they sat by the bar, giving Jonah a few minutes to think about working for the government. After a few minutes passed, they walked back over to Jonah sitting on the upholstered bench facing him on the opposite another side.

"Well, their buddy boy, what do you say? Is it going to be a life of misery or do just a small little job for good old Uncle Sam?"

"Gimme a few minutes, will ya?" Jonah wiped his forehead with his sleeve as he got up and moved to another seat to think things over.

After five minutes passed, giving him a chance to mull it over, he moved back to where they were sitting.

"Details, I need details. Don't leave anything out," Jonah blurted out, feeling as though he was just slammed against the wall.

"Okay! Here ya go. We know that certain items are coming across the borders in Texas, Arizona, and California. There will be an auction somewhere in or near the borders of each state. Our sources tell us that you will be contacted to conduct the sale. What we want from you are information as to when and where the sale will take place. What we need is the items that are going to be sold. That's it, Buddy boy, you in?"

He paused for a few moments before he gave the final answer. What could be so bad? Either the Feds make his life so unbelievably miserable, or he just tells them what they want to know. This isn't too hard of a decision, he thought.

"Yep! I'm in," was Jonah's reply. "What kinds of things or items are coming in, right? After that, we're done, is that correct?"

"Listen, pal, don't sweat it. A deal is a deal. Uncle Sam backs this one. You just give us the info that we want, and you're in the clear. Remember that we need all the info on three sales. They will probably be one right after another, about one or two days apart. Whatever you do, be careful out their buddy boy. These guys are serious, and they'll kill you without batting an eye. We have a man there to protect you, but you should carry a gun with ya anyway. Hey, got any questions for me?" he asked and left without waiting for an answer.

32.

CHAPTER THIRTY-TWO

Within two days after Jonah met with the government agents, a tall, heavy-set man who certainly was well overweight pounded on the door.

"Hombre, anybody home," as he pounded on the door again. Jonah was ready for anything. Sitting at his desk rather nervously with a gun in hand, he shouted, "Doors open," gripping the gun tighter and pulling the hammer back for quick shooting.

As the man opened the door, pushing it open with a loud bang.

"You the man is known as the Auctioneer, Knight?" Jonah didn't have much chance to reply as the man started to talk with a raised voice.

"I was sent here by my boss to tell you that you have to sell some stuff in Texas and maybe a couple of other places. You okay with that? Bet you are hombre."

"I do not work for free. What's the pay?" Jonah asked. "My boss said that he would pay you ten big ones for each sale. You okay with that? You got no choice, hombre. You can pick up thirty big ones. Just do it! You don't want to piss him off. He gets angry if he doesn't get what he wants. Got it?" the man said with a rush and warning tone, leaving no room for Jonah to say anything.

"Okay, okay," was Jonah's reply. Tell me what I'm going to sell, where and when. Also, how do I get there? "

"Don't worry about the small stuff, Hombre; you'll be taken care of, got it? Tomorrow, everything tomorrow. Don't forget to lock up the house. Someone will pick you up and figure that you'll be gone for a few days. The first stop will be near the border near San Diego. I got a farmhouse about 50 miles from the border where the sale will be. Don't talk to anyone, just me or whoever will be with you, got it?"

"Yep," was Jonah's reply. "By the way, when will the sale be, and what is it?" Jonah tried to inquire, he received an answer, "Guns, man, guns, lots of guns and ammo."

"Maybe Houston or somewhere in Texas. I'll let you know, Hombre."

"What's your name?" Jonah asked. Juan, just call me Poncho; everybody does."

"I need to know the exact address of where the sale will take place. I prefer to travel alone if that's okay with you," Jonah replied. "Oh, by the way, I want to get paid after each sale; those are my terms," Jonah said firmly.

"Okay, let me check with my boss, and I'll get back to you pretty quick," Poncho replied.

The following day, Poncho returned at three in the afternoon. "Okay, my boss said that's okay with him. Remember, do not cross him. He really gets angry." Here ya go, Hombre. In Brownsville, Texas, near the docks, there is a warehouse near the fourth street. Really easy to find. Gotta be there in the morning for sale. In Yuma, right near the border, another warehouse is close to the downtown area in the 17th Street warehouse. Ya can't miss it, red brick building in the afternoon and San Diego, well I told you already. Whatever you do, don't be late, got it?" Poncho turned quickly and slammed the door of the house behind him.

He wondered when the feds will contact him to pass the information and be done with this whole business.

On Thursday, as Jonah was ready to leave and drive to Brownsville in his new Oldsmobile four-door Rocket eighty-eight, another man approached him.

"Hey! Do you want to sell me your house? Mind if I come in?" My friend Jeff told me to stop by and talk to you. Do you have the information? Hope so, times a wasting here." "Okay," Jonah replied. "Here ya go," as he passed the handwritten information on to him.

"What's your name?" Jonah asked. "Not important, just listen. Somehow, they think that you're the guy that got his friends killed, and this would be payback. It probably wouldn't happen until the sales were over." He said and further continued, "Carry a loaded gun with you always, and don't worry, a couple of guys from our side will be there as buyers and will watch over you. Take all the precautions that you need. Don't be nervous, or they will think something's wrong. Watch out for everything, got it?" with an alarming raised eyebrow, he quoted, or maybe reminded himself and me of the goal, "We're going to end this guy once and for all. Lots of action; don't forget to duck and run as fast as you can."

Jonah finished putting his duffle bag in the car's trunk and was ready to drive the first sale in Brownsville. It shouldn't take more than eight to ten hours, he thought to himself.

He stopped by a diner to grab a bite to eat when another guy on the road approached him. "Looks like you have been driving for quite a while." Under the counter, the stranger flashed a Federal badge. "We got your back, pal."

"Thanks", was Jonah's reply. "Just want you to feel better about this trip." Without saying another word, he got off the stool and walked out the door.

That's a relief, Jonah thought to himself. After a bathroom break and finishing a meal of eggs, ham, coffee, Jonah went back and continued the drive to the destination.

The warehouse was plain-looking with large doors, lots of chicken-wired windows, and some parking spaces. A few cars rolled up with some scary-looking people. Each car had three or four people in it. Jonah waited until everybody left the cars and then proceeded to walk into the building.

Poncho was waiting for him. "About time you got here," he said with a bellowing voice. "There's the stuff, and all of the people are waiting. Get ready, Knight!"

"I am! Let's start this sale! "Jonah said with a firm, confident voice.

As the bidding began, he got a chill in his bones like something will happen when this sale is over.

There is always grumbling during and after each sale. The hammer fell on a guy that sounded like he was from the south somewhere. This sale brought in two million, which made the boss very happy. He showed up in front of Jonah and, without saying a word, handed

Jonah ten thousand dollars. He was a domineering sight to behold. Even though he was about five-foot-seven tall, everybody did whatever he said. His clothes were the everyday street clothes as not to be noticed in case he had to mingle in any crowd.

"You gonna be in Yuma, right?" he asked. With a sigh of relief, he replied, "that's what you are paying me for, right?"

The boss turned and walked away quickly and headed for his limousine, which quickly drove out of the building.

Jonah started to walk out to his car when there were several gunshots in the building. Jonah ran to his car and drove away quickly. He was scared that he might also be shot. Even though there was a lot of gunfire, he did not want to hang around to see what was happening. *WHEW!* That was close for sure, he thought to himself.

The sale in Yuma was quite a different story. After the sale, one woman took a revolver out of her purse and aimed it directly at Jonah's upper body.

She cocked the trigger and fell to the ground as a federal agent shot her in the head, saving Jonah's life. Before he could thank him, he left the building. Guess that they kept their promise, he thought. Jonah did not go to the sale in San Diego and drove nervously directly home without stopping, except for a bathroom break and some water.

When he arrived home, all he could do was go to bed and try to rest his weary body and calm his nerves.

33.

CHAPTER THIRTY-THREE

Six months later, Jonah and Alexis were enjoying the brightly lit, sun-filled day playing on the beach, laughing, throwing water balloons at each other.

Just being with her together was more than Jonah ever imagined possible. The life he wanted was in front of him. He often dreamed of meeting someone that would take him out of the world of a war-torn, hectic, light and sometimes scary life until he met this beautiful woman. He thought to himself, finally, after years of yearning, his Gravel road is coming to an end. He assumed that with Alexis besides, he would be tormented no more with the past.

He went into the house to refresh the drinks when, from the silence of the day, the shattering ringing sound of the telephone broke the still of the moment. Before the ringing, things were going pretty decent. Upon hearing, Jonah got up to receive the phone with a shuddering heart.

Alexis followed him into the house with a long non-descript look on her face. She looked at him and knowing that this call might be the end of her happiness, for the time being anyway. As she always remembered, the silent job she was hired for, protecting him from all danger so that she could become the final danger for him.

This was her profession. This is what she was trained to do; protect, and assassinate anything or anyone that would get in the way. She was a hired assassin. That was her job.

She knew nothing else. She worked for anyone that would pay her price, not being loyal to anyone. Cold, manipulative, and cunning were the makeup of Alexis Sarkis.

As she followed Jonah to the phone, her mind drifted back, memories echoed in her mind flashing back to when it all started:

Two final shots echoed in the kitchen of the home high in the cliffs of Greece as she lowered the smoking .38, finally coming to rest hanging at her side.

"Done," she thought to herself. Finally, I'm finished with the people that killed her parents. Now, who ordered them killed, she wondered. I will find them and make the kill very painful, yes, painful indeed.

"Kill your prey, and you will be rewarded," they would say.

"Never let anything gets in the way of your job. Always remember, never look back, leave as quickly as you came," she was told. "Kill and get out."

Alexis was always taught to obey her employer no matter what.

Alexis was an exceptional child. Since she was four, her parents started to teach her about life, keeping her from asking too many questions about what they do. Sometimes they would be gone for a week, and the babysitter or most commonly known as her protector, would come and stay with her. The protector knew what to do in case someone tried to kidnap or harm this child.

Physically, she was very strong, trying to always pick fights with her classmates, mostly the boys, to show what she could really do. Everybody in the school wanted to be her friend so others would not bully them.

She would ask a lot of questions about where they went and what they did. Finally, when she was nine years old, they broke down and started to teach her about sports equipment, how they work and how to use the various items to cause harm to other people.

Her parents died in an accident when their Mercedes Benz suddenly drove off a cliff when she was only fourteen years old. They were driving over the high mountain road around the city when the brakes gave way. Someone had cut the brake lines so the fluid would slowly leak out as they tumbled down the cliff to their ultimate demise.

They were known as the choice to commit murder without being traced. With each kill, they would disappear into the world without a trace. They were the best at the job.

Both were known in the underworld as the "Poison Pair."

She was born on the island of Crete near the Aegean Sea, the largest of the Greek Islands, where their parents started their cruel and vicious killing for hire business.

Alexis always was curious about everything and was especially good at reading.

She was an excellent all-around student. She was excellent at all form's athletics, including Archery, which she will use in the future of her not yet found career. She wanted to know everything, including the use of firearms and explosives.

Her parents taught her the use of all types of weapons, starting at the ripe age of eleven. They kept her from the general population for her own safety and protection, fully knowing that someone would be trying to get even by killing someone they loved very much. When they went to the mainland, they wore disguises for protection and, of course, to meld into the crowds.

When her parents were killed, she knew that they had to be revenged. She knew the people who did it. She knew exactly what to do. All the Kooris family was well known around the island and were feared. They hated her parents, often mentioning that they would kill them if they were paid for it. They terrorized everyone and would stomp out anyone that got in their way.

Two weeks later, Alexis had her plan put together. She was loading up with a bow, arrow, and two of her parent's revolvers equipped with a silencer attached. She went to the house where they were living, watching them laughing through the bushes as they drank Ouzo.

These people will not be laughing for long; she thought no, not for long. Alexis dressed in her school clothing, loaded her school bag with two guns with attached silencers screwed tightly on the barrels, so the kills would be silent.

Going to the door, she rang the bell. The middle-aged woman answered, "Can I help you?" she said when the door opened.

"I'm looking for the Sarkis family. Do you know where they live?"

"Sure, common in," the woman said, I'll point out the house. You can see it from the kitchen window."

As they were walking towards the room, she looked around at the large rooms in the house, finding the opportunity to fulfill her mission.

She was going to kill everyone in the house for what they did to her parents, she promised to herself.

She followed her into the kitchen and promptly placed a bullet directly into her skull as she was pointing out the window. Lexi held her as not to make any noise as her body fell on the floor.

Quietly she crept out into the large room where there was Spiro, the head of the family, smoking a large cigar, sitting on the large sofa with his feet up on the ottoman, looking out the large window at sea.

Taking careful aim, she shot his foot which would cripple him for a short time. His yelling in pain brought the remaining three members of the household into the room.

As they entered, two of them were holding a small firearm, and one carried a sawed-off shotgun.

Lexi hid on the side of a wall where she could see everything. Taking careful aim, she fatally shot two and shot the other one in the leg. Lexi rolled on the floor, where she quickly shot the felled man through the heart.

One at a time, she hit her mark, directly through the heart with the force strength of a madman. With each kill, she yelled, "THIS WAS FOR MY PARENTS."

Lexi knew who planned it and saved him for the last.

"Do you want to live, old man?" She asked.

"Please, don't kill me. I'll do anything," Spiro said, "anything."

"Who do you work for, and I want a list of all your clients, or I'll kill you now. Who ordered my parents to be killed?" She demanded.

He pointed to the desk in the corner, "Push the bottom panel. There is a door with everything you want," Spiro said with moans from the shot he sustained.

Lexi pushed the panel where a hidden secret door popped open.

Everything you want is there. Let me go, please," he begged.

"Who ordered my parents to be killed," she demanded again loudly.

"Figure it out for yourself, bitch," he said as he lunged toward the gun, turning quickly, she emptied the final bullet into his chest.

Now she knows who the enemy is and who she can work with. At fourteen years old, Alexis Sarkis now has a very profitable business with one less competition to deal with.

Some day she will get them all, one at a time, until she finds out who ordered the kill, she thought. They will pay for what they did. Everyone will pay.

Lexi reviewed the book carefully, making notes as to the contents, noting names, phone numbers, and addresses. Putting the book in her backpack, she left the house —all dead with no trace that she was ever there.

Her parents taught her well, yes indeed. Alexis will be the new assassin that will make a lot of money doing what she was taught.

She now has the list of the people that will hire her to do their dirty work. Kill, poison, death by arrow, strangulation, and any other devices that she can conjure up. She would stop at nothing to protect or kill her assignment.

A new killer has risen and entered the world of mayhem.

34.

CHAPTER THIRTY-FOUR

Alexis never thought or ever planned she would fall in love with this man named Jonah Knight. The phone ringing reminded her that it was time to polish and clean her revolvers and be ready for anything.

Jonah never thought that he would be found. He tried to conceal, cover his tracks.

He wanted to vanish and disappear off the face of the earth.

Secretly knowing that if someone wanted him, there would be nowhere, he could hide.

Again, with each ring, it sounded like an explosion rocking his world. They stared at one another, expressionless.

After several rings, Alexis reached out, grabbing his hand as he reached for the receiver.

"I'll get it," she said. "Hello, hello? Yes, Yes, I understand, sorry."

She hung up the phone with a smile on her face, so Jonah wouldn't think anything was wrong.

"That was the desk, something about food. Ha, would you know it, wrong room?"

"Be right back, honey, gotta go to the bathroom. I'll meet you outside, okay?"

"Sure thing," he said. "Meet you down by the water."

Jonah felt a bit suspicious about the call echoing in his mind were the words of Flagstaff, "Do not trust anybody as your life depends upon it." Since when did the desk call? A strange and uneasy feeling came over him. His gut feelings were telling him of imminent danger. His stomach started to turn nervously as if it was a warning buzzer going off.

Did they find him? Questions were running rampant, over and over in his mind. Be on guard, he thought to himself. Be careful, no matter what. Just to be safe, he went outside, cautiously looking around for anything that was out of place or strange. Slowly he moved around the building, leaning against the corner, and waited silently.

Alexis, wearing a blue and white beach coat, covered herself up, walked out with her hands in her pocket.

"Jonah, my love, where are you?" speaking with her raised melodious voice.

Alexis slowly pulled out a small Smith & Wesson .38 caliber snub nose to complete her assignment. The voice at the other end of the phone was the command. The voice whispered, "You know what you have to do. Do it now!" and hung up.

All the good times are at the end. Her job, her mission is almost over. After all, she is a trained assassin hired to do a job. Alexis Sarkis was very well trained in the art of murder and mayhem.

"Kill your prey, and you will be rewarded. Never let anything get in the way of your job! Kill and get out, never look back," kept echoing in her mind.

"Jonah, where are you," she asked again, walking out onto the porch. Jonah saw the gun holding steadily in her hand as she moved across the porch cautiously. He knew at that moment it was over. All the time that she was gone were assignments, and now he was her assignment. She was clearly going to kill him. Jonah was her target and no one else's.

Quickly, he flung his arm out and knocked the gun out of her hand, letting it fall on the sand. He has never seen such fury from her eyes like this. They were the scariest he had ever seen.

Alexis lunged at him, throwing them both down, rolling off the porch and onto the sand. Her hands were clenching his neck, squeezing, pushing her thumbs deep into his throat as tight as she possibly could.

Jonah was gasping for air, trying to reach for the gun that was just beyond his grasp.

She was a very strong athletic woman with more power beyond some men.

Reaching, stretching the fingers on his left hand, and just barely touching the gun, all the while trying to get a full grip on her hands so he could breathe. Gasping for air, his breathing getting shallower as she squeezed tighter. Her teeth were clenched tightly, smiling, saying coldly, "Die, my love, die, die!"

Choking, gasping for more air, suddenly she loosened her grip, collapsing on top of him; blood was running out of a hole in her chest. A man was running towards him with a gun-waving in the air.

Ready to reshoot her to make sure she was dead. Jonah coughed, choking, holding his throat, trying to catch his breath.

Jonah stabilized himself and leaned over while kneeling over her bleeding body, cradling her in his arms

"Why?" he asked, "Why?"

"You were my job, but I fell in love with you. I'm sorry," she said as she reached into her beach coat for the other revolver.

The strange man quickly shot her again, pinning the shot square in her forehead, finally taking the remaining breath out of her.

Coughing, "Who are you," Jonah asked.

"I'm one of the Watchmen. We were keeping an eye on you all the time, Knight. Especially the last two months. This woman was very, very dangerous. We heard through the grapevine that she was going to do something drastic. Lucky for you, we got here as soon as we could.

You have a very influential and powerful friend. This guy must like you very much."

"Who is it, may I ask?" Jonah asked.

"Don't know for sure. All I know is that he is very rich and powerful. Usually, whatever he says, goes. He's quite a guy, lucky you."

Staring down at the body with sadness, "This broad was a well-trained assassin, ya know. A killer for hire, or you can say a regular killing machine. She was known all over in the right circles and quite deadly. She was a very dangerous chick to be with. Careful, Knight, better be more careful in the future."

"Thanks, thank you very much," he stuttered, Jonah said, stammering as he continued to stare at the lifeless body of the woman he loved. He was still unable to realize what happened, partially in denial.

"No time for that. Help me put her in the boat, quick," he ordered.

"Hey, get her clothes, makeup, and all of that shit out of the house and put them in the boat with her. Move Knight. No time to waste, move it," the man shouted.

Both men carried her into the small speed boat anchored just shy of the beach, laying her on the bottom with all her clothes, covering her up with a light tan-colored canvas tarpaulin. The Watchman proceeded to pour gasoline all over her limp body and the cloth covering her, flooding the boat with the rest of the flammable liquid.

He tied the steering wheel tightly, pointing straight out into the open waters. He started the engine, turning the bow toward the vastness of the ocean, letting it warm up for a moment. The man opened the Zippo lighter, striking the wheel bringing up the high flame, and tossed it in the boat, igniting the gas.

Reaching in, he pulled the throttle all the way back.

The bow raised high, heading for the sky as it sped out into the Atlantic. After a moment of high flames, the boat exploded with splinters flying in every direction, shattering the boat into several pieces. Her body was torn apart with the explosion, giving the sharks food for the day. The body Jonah held so many times in his arm. Just like her killings were never heard of, she too won't be heard by anyone. Alexis, the assassin, will kill no more.

Both men went over and picked up the blood-soaked sand with a small shovel placing it into a pail, walking it down to the seashore.

"The waters will dissolve the blood," the Watchman said. "A shark can smell blood from pretty far away."

"Here's a bag. Wrap up anything left. Make sure you have everything. Carry it a couple of miles down the road and dump it, got it?"

"Wait a minute, he said, why don't you have a bonfire instead. Burn everything. Throw out the Just burn 'em, gather the ashes, and crunch them up into something that the wind will carry away. "

"Go home, Knight. It's time you went home for a while," the watchman said. "Check up on your house and relax. Whatever you do, don't come back here. Too many people already know about this place. Whatever you do, don't answer the phone or talk to people that you don't know. Go it? You will be watched, got it? See ya, pal," he said as he walked off the beach to a waiting white Cadillac convertible and sped away quickly.

Jonah went back to the house, packed up everything, getting it ready for the fire doing exactly what he was told.

He cleaned up everything, being careful not to leave any traces that he was ever there.

Upon walking out the door, the silence was broken by the ring of the phone, "Yes?" he said abruptly. What did I do, he thought? He told me not to answer the phone. Instinct, I guess.

Finally, after several rings, Jonah picked up the receiver. Silence on the other end, "Hello," again he said more sternly. The sound on the other end was that of a woman with a heavy foreign accent, "Meister Knights? Is this Meister Jonas Knights?"

"No, he is not here. He left a few hours ago." Slamming the phone down on the cradle. How familiar this was to him. How did they find me? I did everything I could to hide. Done, I'm done with all of this, he thought. "Once in, never out," echoed in his mind.

The telephone continued to ring and ring again and again. He picked up the phone on the fifth ring, "Yeah?"

"Your services are needed immediately, Mr. Knights. Don't leave; my men will be there to pick you up in a few minutes," she said in the deep feminine baritone voice on the other end, hanging up the phone.

Moments later before he could leave the cottage, there was a loud knock at the door. Two heavy set, muscular men pushed their way in. Each man was wearing a white tropical shirt with a noticeable bulge on the side.

"Grab your everything and let's go Knight, no time to waste. We gotta catch a plane." Without hesitating, the men grabbed his suitcase and took his arm and proceeded to drag him out the door.

Jonah thought that his gravel road finally came to an end when it is going to begin again. Flagstaff was right, once in, never out.

www.ingramcontent.com/pod-product-compliance
Lightning Source LLC
Chambersburg PA
CBHW060624260626
47161CB00008B/2793